LOVED BY
You

M.L. YOUNG

D1523295

INTRODUCTION

This book features alternating points of view. Each chapter is titled with the character whose point of view you are reading from.

Want to receive the first three volumes of my serial series The Stipulation for free? Sign up for my mailing list below and have them delivered right to your inbox. You'll receive new book notifications, free books, giveaways, and much more!

http://eepurl.com/bb6VVb

TABLE OF CONTENTS

CHAPTER ONE	1
CHAPTER TWO	7
CHAPTER THREE	24
CHAPTER FOUR	28
CHAPTER FIVE	36
CHAPTER SIX	41
CHAPTER SEVEN	48
CHAPTER EIGHT	57
CHAPTER NINE	62
CHAPTER TEN	72
CHAPTER ELEVEN	79
CHAPTER TWELVE	95
CHAPTER THIRTEEN	99
CHAPTER FOURTEEN	122
CHAPTER FIFTEEN	127
CHAPTER SIXTEEN	138
CHAPTER SEVENTEEN	143
CHAPTER EIGHTEEN	149
CHAPTER NINETEEN	153
CHAPTER TWENTY	165
CHAPTER TWENTY-ONE	173
CHAPTER TWENTY-TWO	184
CHAPTER TWENTY-THREE	187
ABOUT THE AUTHOR	191

CHAPTER ONE

Blake

A whirlwind had surrounded and enveloped me and I wasn't sure I could see past the swirling smoke that had engulfed my life.

Why was everything in life so difficult? One minute I could be on cloud nine with the woman who I knew I whole-heartedly wanted to be with, and the next minute I could be sitting alone in my apartment wondering what in the fuck even happened.

I had no clue what to think about what Penelope had laid on me. I knew I was disappointed—a little mad, even, but why? Did I not do something similar to her before? Did I not use her for my own selfish gain? Sure, mine wasn't financial, obviously, but I still used her for something that I wanted and it fucked everything up. Now she'd done the same thing to me, albeit a tiny bit different, and she was in the place I was long ago.

As I walked around my apartment, I walked over to my wine fridge and pulled out a bottle of Merlot. Uncorking it, a loud thump went off before I pulled a glass out of the cabinet and tilted it on its side. The red nectar flowed out before I twisted the bottle gently and stopped the flow. I set the bottle on the counter and swirled my glass around gently before pulling it up to my nose and smelling it. My mouth began to salivate and my taste buds puckered before I took my first sip, a small sip, and set the glass back down on the counter. I put my hands against the edge and looked out towards the city.

Why did I feel like I was in such an impossible position? I knew I wasn't, or at least I thought I wasn't, but I couldn't help but feel let down and a bit ashamed. Did my behavior prompt all of this? Penelope wasn't the type of person to use someone. She would never just go and do that to somebody unless they did something to her first. To be honest, I was surprised that she even chose to do any of this in the first place. She didn't seem like that type of girl.

Did I dare go back for more? I wanted to, I knew that, but there had to be changes—and big ones. There couldn't be any more secrets, and there couldn't be a veiled mystique surrounding us. I knew things about Penelope, good things, but I needed to know more if I were to ever make things work. She needed to know more about me as well. Here I was, ready to commit to this girl, ready to give her my all, and I didn't even know her middle name. I didn't know her friends, her family, or her life story before I met her. Sure, I knew some of it, but not all of it. If I was going to make this work, I needed us to know one another and be able to be honest and open about all aspects of our lives. I knew that meant opening up about everything and everyone who had come into my life, including the one who made me who I am today, even though I never wanted to speak of her again. I guess that would just be a small price to pay for eternal happiness.

I walked over to the table and picked my phone up. I unlocked it, seeing I had a few messages from work, but nothing from her. I hesitated, wondering if I should even take the risk and send her something right now, or if I should just wait a day or two so that things could die down. No, I couldn't wait any longer. I couldn't go through the misery of waiting while I knew we should be talking and rekindling things.

I opened my messages and wandered over to her thread, seeing all of our interactions there. I scrolled up and down through them, reading the happy and flirty moments together like I was reading them for the first time again. A picture was there, a goofy one of her making a face, and I couldn't help but smile and let out a small laugh as I felt something inside me. I always felt something inside me when I saw her face. I couldn't explain it, but it was definitely there, and I couldn't forget it.

I started typing, not even sure what I was really saying, before I hit send and looked at it. I didn't say all that much, nothing special, but I let her know that I wanted to talk to her. I let her know that things could be fixed, even if I didn't really say that directly. I implied it, and that was all that mattered.

I set my phone down, walked back over to the counter, and took a big swig of my Merlot instead of the small sip I'd taken earlier. I needed something to take the tension out of this. I needed to feel calm. After all, what if she wrote back that she was finished with me? What if she hated my guts and didn't give me that chance to get to know her better? I knew I was overreacting, and that things weren't *that* bad, but when you put yourself out there, you sometimes have a little cloud of doubt following you.

My phone buzzed on the table, just a short vibrate. I set down my glass and walked over towards the table. I took a deep breath as I walked, the alcohol vapor expelling out of me, as I grabbed my phone and unlocked it. She'd messaged me back.

"*I didn't know if I was going to hear from you,*" she said.

"*You didn't think I was stupid enough to give you up, did you?*" I replied hesitantly.

"*I'm not sure,*" she said.

"*I don't want to lose out on something that has the potential to be great. I think we need to see each other in person for this, though. I have some things I need to say, and some conditions that need to be set if this is going to work out,*" I said.

"*The last time there were conditions on our relationship, arrangement, or whatever you want to call it, things went horribly wrong,*" she replied.

"*They aren't anything like that, I swear. They need to be done, though. Just trust me. Please?*"

"*...fine. I'll trust you on this, but you better not let me down. How about tomorrow?*" she asked.

I sent her details and she said she'd see me tomorrow before leaving the conversation to do some homework. I felt relieved but a bit scared at the same time. What if this wasn't really what she wanted? What if she didn't want to share her past with me for fear that these things would happen all over again? She had every right to feel that way, and it scared me half to death. I couldn't go through messing up with her again. It wasn't an option.

I finished another small glass of wine before walking upstairs and getting ready for bed. As I splashed some warm water on my face and looked up at myself in the crystal-clear mirror, I couldn't help but notice the small bit of relief on my face. It definitely wasn't there this morning, and for good reason. Things were going to change, though, I knew it, and I knew we would get through anything. The only problem was facing the demons of my past that I wondered if I'd ever release again. You can tell a lot about a man by his past, his upbringing, though I wasn't sure exposing Penelope to that was the best choice. I knew I had to, but I sure as hell didn't have to want to.

I slipped into my pajama pants, took off my shirt, and walked over to my bed as the small bedside lamp illuminated a small section of my room. With one last glance over the city, I crawled underneath the covers and pulled them up to my chest. I cleared my throat, looked up at the ceiling, and took a breath before turning off the lamp and exposing myself to the darkness. No matter what things popped up, no matter what she heard or she saw, I knew that I could keep her. I had to keep her. She was the one person I knew, the only person, who would accept everything about my past and never use it against me. I could trust her, I knew that.

I closed my eyes, a million thoughts racing through my mind, and tried my hardest to fall asleep fast.

Tomorrow had a lot in store for me—I knew it.

CHAPTER TWO

Penelope

I awoke to a screeching ambulance barreling down the street outside my bedroom window. I squinted, letting out a small moan as I did so, before grabbing my phone and looking at the time.

I had ten minutes before I had to wake up, and I couldn't have been more annoyed that I wasn't given those precious minutes with my eyes closed and my mind completely shut down. Not wanting to tempt fate and sleep past my alarm, I yawned, unlocked my phone, and read my e-mail and social media before finally getting up and stretching as I sat on the edge of my bed.

I took a sip of water from the cup on my nightstand and got up as I turned off my two alarms and picked out some clothes for the day. I wasn't going to shower, only wash my face and brush my teeth, as I had class before I had to go and meet Blake. I was definitely going to get myself prepared before then, since this was a big deal and all, and I was even going to wash my hair for him, which as a woman is a *huge* deal. This puffball doesn't just dry quickly, after all. It takes taming.

Nicolette was already gone when I walked out in the living room. I think she had a hot yoga class before work or something like that. She said some girl from work invited her, and she felt too bad to say no. I think going to a hot yoga class before work is almost body-odor suicide, but I guess she didn't care all that much.

I splashed some warm water on my face and used my grapefruit face wash, the little chunks in it scrubbing away my dead skin cells. I felt refreshed, rejuvenated, and most of all, ready for the day. After applying a conservative amount of makeup, I put my hair up into a small bun and got changed. Nothing special, as I was only going to some classes, after all, but it was good enough.

I'd spent the entire night studying for a small test I had today, which unfortunately meant I wasn't able to talk to Blake outside of our small conversation over text. I still couldn't believe that he wanted to talk to me and see me after what I did. Sure, some people would think it wasn't all that bad, but to me, it was. I felt as if I'd betrayed him, and even though he originally did that to me, and I knew I shouldn't even feel the slightest bit of nervousness, I did. I was just happy we were going to be able to move past all of this and start fresh like we should've done the first time. At least I hoped those were his intentions. If he played me again I wasn't sure that I'd ever be able to go back. Fool me twice, shame on me.

The bus was pulling up to the stop as I ran around the corner, completely out of breath, and got in line. There were four people in front of me, all of them older. Each one of them swiped their cards and found an empty seat. After swiping mine and looking around the crowded bus, I noticed not a single seat was available, as none of the other riders even looked up at me and were instead engrossed in their phones or tablets.

I gripped a handrail above and planted my feet firmly as I swayed back and forth each and every time the bus turned a corner or stopped completely. After a little while, I happily got off and felt my hand still a little clenched; I knew it was likely red and throbbing underneath my gloves. I hated standing on the bus with an ever-burning passion.

As I walked into the building, I felt my phone buzz in my pocket and took it out to see that Blake had messaged me. I smiled, unlocking my phone, and waited as my eyes adjusted enough from the brightness outside to see my dimly lit screen.

"*Feel like meeting where it all began tonight?*" he asked.

"*I think I could swing that. What time?*" I replied.

"*Eight. We won't have the place to ourselves, but I promise some seclusion so that we can talk. Would you like me to send Gustav?*" he asked.

"*Don't trouble him. I'll get there, don't worry,*" I replied.

"*Great. I'll see you there,*" he said, with a smiley face at the end.

I bit my lower lip and put my phone away before walking into my classroom and putting my stuff down. I took out a bottle of water from my bag and sipped on it a little as the icy cold liquid inside shocked my somewhat sensitive teeth. I was so excited to see him tonight. I'd wondered a lot and asked myself many times if I should've even told him the things that I'd done before. If I hadn't, there wouldn't be any makeup dinner, if that was even what this was. We'd be together already and loving life with one another. I could've said yes and become his girlfriend, and my life would have been pure and utter bliss. I guess having a conscience didn't always help with those things.

My communications class, the last one I'd ever take, wasn't remotely fun or interesting. In fact, I mostly daydreamed while I was in here and still did okay, though I guess I did study a lot. I guess I only had to study a lot because I never paid attention, and I would just not come altogether if I could, but attendance was ten percent of our grades and I wasn't willing to get a B just because I was too lazy to come sit for an hour.

"I'll soon be passing out your exams. Please feel free to take the entire class period to take it, and once you're done you may bring it up to me and leave. Are there any questions?" my professor asked.

She looked around the room as not a single hand went up before saying good, nodding, and grabbing a stack of thick packets and handing them out one by one. She used an anti-cheating method, which involved her manually handing out exams so she could give different versions of the same exam to different people. That way the person sitting next to you had their questions in a different order and you couldn't copy off them. Pretty genius, but I think it added a lot more work for her.

I gave her a polite smile and took my test from her as I flipped through the few pages to see how many questions there were. There were forty in all, some short, some long, though all of them were intense. I wrote my name and class section at the top and put the butt of my pencil up to my lips as I read the first question.

People all around me were scribbling their answers like they had a gun held up to their heads as I casually took my time and thought over each question. I had a little over a minute to answer each one, and I planned to use *all* of that time.

One by one, each student got up and handed in their exams as I trudged on and tried my hardest. I knew a lot of the answers, mostly the fill-in-the-blanks, though some of the multiple choice ones were a little difficult. I wondered if she went over this in class, but then again I was never really that mentally awake during her classes. I guess there's something about a monotone voice that just doesn't make you want to listen all that much.

With five minutes left on the clock, I reached my final question, an easier one, as I confidently wrote in the answer and closed my test. I put away my things, picked them up, and walked up to the front where she was grading some of the exams that had already been turned in. She nodded and I set mine down on top of her pile and walked out of the classroom and into the empty hallway. I pulled out my phone, saw a low signal, and walked towards a sub shop in the student center that had a deal on foot-longs.

I grabbed a turkey and provolone with every vegetable they had, handed the guy six bucks, and walked over to the tables with my bottle of water and started to eat. Other students whizzed by me, likely on their way to their next classes, as I finally took a breather and watched the world outside of the frosty windows directly in front of me. I just hoped tonight went as smoothly as today had.

"So, he took you back?" Nicolette asked as I got ready later that night.

"Not yet, at least I don't think so. He wants to talk things out, but I have hope for it. He contacted me," I said.

"Wow, that's great. And to think, you thought you'd never hear from him again. I guess things worked out better than you thought, huh?" she asked.

"I sure hope so. I guess we'll find out soon. How do I look?" I asked, modeling myself for her.

"Good, but here," she said, grabbing some hair spray and moving my hair around a little.

I closed my eyes as I was enveloped in the sticky mist that clouded around me. She soon finished, and

I slowly opened my eyes and looked in the mirror. My hair looked better, sexier, and my black dress hugged my hips and accented my cleavage. I turned around, looking at myself from every angle as I did so, before accepting what I saw and going to get my shoes.

"What are you going to do tonight?" I asked as I picked them up and put them on.

"Not too much. I might watch something on Netflix, not sure. I suppose the night is ahead of me to do whatever I want with it," she said.

"Please stay off the app tonight. I don't think it's working so well for you anymore," I said.

"I can't go away just because of one bad experience. Besides, that guy was nuts. I'll be fine," she said.

"Whatever you say," I replied in a not-so-happy voice.

I grabbed my purse and shoved everything inside that I always brought with me when I went to see Blake. I was hoping that he'd ask me to come over, have a glass of wine, and cuddle with him all night, but I wasn't counting on it. I knew that things might be a little tense, so I just wanted to make sure we were kosher instead of hoping for anything more.

"Well, have a good time. I won't wait up for you," Nicolette said.

"I hope you won't have to," I said, smiling, before walking out the door.

There was a bus that went close to where the restaurant was. After waiting outside in the cold, my legs becoming a little too cold for comfort, the bus came around the corner as the exhaust billowed out in a cloud of smoke. I got on, swiped my card, and got a seat before we took off down the road.

As we got closer to the restaurant, I felt butterflies build up in my stomach as they tickled my insides and made me more nervous than I'd been in a while. Hell, I wasn't even this nervous when I told him I'd been lying to him. I guess maybe I knew that this was the last chance. If we couldn't make it work now, on our third attempt, then it would never happen. I didn't want that to happen. I wanted to be with him, I wanted to be his, and I wanted to make it work more than anything. I still had hope, huge hope, but I hoped that he felt the same way.

The bus let off near the restaurant and an older woman and I both got off. With a cool breeze rolling my way, I pulled my coat up to my mouth and walked towards the door of the restaurant. Their parking lot was filled, including Blake's car, and another person was pulling in. The door was opened for me as the welcome warmth inside crashed against my likely reddened skin.

"Good evening, madam. Do you have a reservation?" the maître d' asked.

"I'm here to see somebody. He should be here already," I said.

"Name, please?"

"Hunter. Blake Hunter," I said.

"Oh, yes, Ms. Wells, we've been expecting you. Please, if you'll follow me, I'll escort you to his table," the man said.

We walked through the small open lane for

traffic as I was led towards the back of the restaurant. After walking through curtains, there he was. Blake, who was sitting at a table sipping ice water, smiled before standing up.

"I'll take it from here. Thank you, Pierre," Blake said.

"As you wish, sir," Pierre said before leaving.

"How are you?" I asked as I went in for a hug.

"A little better now that you're here," he replied, kissing me on the cheek.

I felt my cheeks get warm as I got shivers up and down my spine. Things were already looking good, and I couldn't be happier.

"Please, sit. We have a lot to talk about tonight," he said.

I took off my coat and hung it on a hook next to his outside the booth before sitting down across from him. I took a sip of water from the crystal glass in front of me.

"So, how have you been?" he asked.

"Okay, I guess. Just a lot of schoolwork. Nothing really too exciting, though I guess my life never is. How about you?" I asked.

"Well, I just got back the other day from a quick business trip. I suppose those never stop, which may or may not be a good thing. I've missed you," he said.

"I've missed you," I said, smiling.

"I think things have changed for me ever since I met you, Penny. You've had this huge effect on me, and I don't even know how to explain it. I wish I could, but I don't know the right words or where to even begin," he said.

"You don't have to. I think I know what you mean," I said.

Blake was such a different man from the first time I met him. He was more open, caring, and definitely more trusting. Was I the person who'd changed him, or was it something natural that just came out? I'd hoped that I was the one who'd had some kind of effect on him, but you never know.

"I didn't think that you were ever going to contact me again. I thought that I blew it," I said.

"No, you didn't. I think I just needed a little time to cool down and reevaluate everything in my life. Things have been different ever since you came along, and it's not that different is bad, not even close to it, but it's just…*different*," he said.

"Yeah, I know what you mean. I used to wonder if I'd ever find that one person or get that happiness that I always see other people having. I was never the girl who got hit on or talked to or anything like that. I was just like this shadow to my friends whenever we went out. So having something different, especially with you, is good," I said.

"Yes, it is," he said, smiling.

"Hello, how are you two doing this evening?" a woman said as she walked up with two menus.

"I'm doing well, and yourself?" Blake asked.

"Marvelous, thanks for asking. May I start you off with a drink, maybe an appetizer?" the waitress asked.

"I think we'll take a bottle of red, please. Whatever your finest one is. Would you like an appetizer?" Blake asked, looking at me.

As I looked at the menu, I saw garlic-infused green beans and my mouth started to salivate. I used to eat those, at least something like them, as a kid and hadn't had them in years.

"The green beans, please," I said, smiling.

"Great, I'll get that right in and be back with your wine," she said before walking away.

"I hope that's okay," I said, looking at him.

"Of course it is. You're fine," he said as he reached out across the table and grabbed my hands.

I looked him in the eyes and saw his softened expression. Here he was, the man of my dreams, right across from me, and I couldn't help but smile and laugh like a schoolgirl. Even after all this, even after everything we'd gone through and the hellish flames that had tried to burn us away from one another, we were still here smiling and being close to one another. I didn't know what I did in a past life to deserve this, but I was glad I did.

"So, I wanted to talk to you about something tonight. It's part of the reason why I asked you here," he said.

"Okay, shoot," I said nervously.

"Well, I was just thinking a lot about us and getting together. Not only that, but the stuff we've already been through. I like you, I really do, but I think if we're going to give this another shot then we need to do it a little differently," he said.

I froze with nervousness and trepidation, as I hadn't a clue what he was talking about. Obviously we had to do things a little differently, like not trying to mess with one another and use the other person in any way, but it almost seemed like he wasn't going in that direction; he should've already known that and known that I knew that too.

"What do you mean, exactly?" I asked.

"Well, how much do we really know about one another? We're comfortable around one another, and we trust one another and have a great time, but we don't even know each other's middle names or favorite anything. I think that if we're going to do this, we need to take it seriously and need to really put everything into it. I want to build something with you, not short-term, but long-term," he said.

"Really?" I asked.

"Really," he replied.

I had to admit that I was in full and utter shock. Blake had never really asked a whole lot about my past, my upbringing, or even the types of things that I liked, but I guess I never asked him either. We were just two people who really liked one another, but without any proper basis for relationship success. He was right that if we were going to make this work for the long haul, we needed to be connected on a much deeper level.

"Nicole," I said, taking him by surprise.

"What?" he asked.

"My middle name. You said you didn't know it. It's Nicole," I said.

"Penelope Nicole Wells. I like it. Mine is David," he said.

"It's cute, like you," I said, and he smirked.

"Okay, here we are," our waitress, whose nametag I saw read Beatriz, said as she came back.

With a food runner helping her, she set down the green beans and two plates on the table before pulling out the wine bottle from the chiller. Blake approved the bottle, and she poured some for him to taste before he agreed and asked for the entire thing, which must've shocked her a little. It's not every day that you have a man buying an almost five-thousand-dollar bottle of wine.

She poured our glasses and set them down before asking if we were ready to order, which we were. Blake ordered the steak, medium-rare, and I ordered the chicken with roasted vegetables and cream sauce. Beatriz took our menus and smiled before walking away past the curtain and leaving us once again in solitude.

I took a sip of my wine and it made me pucker my lips a bit from the shock to my taste buds. Still holding hands, Blake and I kept our gaze on one another as our relationship, which was definitely back on, seemed to instantly go even further than I'd ever hoped. I knew it was a small step, but I also knew it was an important one.

"How is it?" I asked as Blake bit into his steak.

Juice dripped off of his bite when he raised it to his mouth and I couldn't help but feel a little jealous, even though my dish was very juicy too. He chewed for a couple seconds, swallowed, and then looked at me with a smile.

"Like butter. I love it," he said, cutting off another small bite.

I cut into my chicken breast and the white sauce parted around it as I pierced it with my fork and lifted it up to my mouth. Steam billowed upwards before I blew it on a little as to not burn my tongue. I took the bite, the snap of the cheesy, creamy sauce pressing against my taste buds, and my mouth was coated in a wonderment of chickeny goodness. It was almost like sex, though maybe a bit better. I wouldn't tell Blake that, though.

"So, what's your favorite movie?" Blake asked.

"Hm, I'm not sure. I guess *The Notebook*. Kind of dumb, huh? The quintessential girl movie," I said.

"Not stupid at all. I'd never say you were stupid for liking something. I'd have to say mine is *Rocky*. I don't know why, but I've loved that movie since I was a kid," he said.

"Wasn't that out long before, though?" I asked.

"Long before I was a kid? Yeah, it was, but my friend down the street had it on tape and we used to watch it almost every weekend, sometimes twice in a row. The raw, unadulterated machismo and simple yet powerful narrative just screamed to my young, impressionable mind."

"I like this—talking to you and finding out more about you," I said.

"It's nice. It's almost too bad that we couldn't have had this all along. We were too focused on the wrong things, I think," he said.

"Well, all that's important is that we have it now. Better late than never, right?" I asked.

Blake nodded before taking a sip of his wine and swirling it around a little in his glass. There he was, with a dripping steak and side of garlic mashed potatoes, sipping an expensive glass of wine, and I couldn't help but be completely infatuated with him. He wasn't doing anything special, far from it, but he had this air about him that I couldn't help but feel. He made me feel calm and collected, but most of all, he made me feel loved.

We took our time with the rest of the dinner and even opted for some chocolate fondue for dessert before Blake paid the check and we sat there, both of us likely thinking about our next move, as I anxiously waited to see if he was going to ask me back to his place or end the night now. I was fine with either, but after how well our date went, I wanted to go back. I didn't care about sex; I just wanted to be with him for another night. To feel his warm, hard body against mine and know that I was safe.

"Would you like to come back to my place? I know that might sound a bit sudden, but I'd really hate for this most perfect of nights to end already," Blake said.

And then, in a flash, I felt the warmth of happiness envelop me as my nerves and trepidation seemed to vanish almost instantly.

"I'd love to. You aren't being too sudden at all. I'd hate for this night to end as well," I said with a smile.

"Great. Shall we go?" he asked as he got up and grabbed my coat.

I stood up before he helped me into my coat and

I buttoned myself up. I wasn't ready to face the cold yet again, but a leather-wrapped car with heated seats sure helped the situation.

The staff was very friendly and thanked us for coming in before we walked outside past a few people smoking to his car. He opened the door for me and helped me inside, and I smelled the sweet Italian leather. Blake got into the driver's seat and started her up as the engine instantly came on and roared like a monster from some biblical tale.

As we drove to his place I saw people taking out their phones and taking pictures of the car as we pulled up to stops and waited to go. I leaned down a little, not wanting to be photographed, though I was sure their cameras weren't powerful enough to break through tinted windows in the dark. It wasn't that I hated being seen with him, or in this car, but rather that I just hated having the focus on me. It was something I'd never been comfortable with since I was a kid.

As we sat at the last stop before his building, he looked over at me, his eyes locking with mine. We didn't say a single word, though thousands were said without so much as a peep. This felt right, this felt good, and most importantly, this felt safe.

Blake pressed the button for his garage and we slowly pulled in over the bump as the door closed behind us. People walked past it before it bolted itself down and Blake drove up to his special car elevator. As the door opened he pulled all the way inside and we were slowly lifted up all those stories to the top of his building, where his apartment waited patiently.

"Here we are," he said as the elevator stopped and the doors opened behind us.

We got out, walked inside his place, and I instantly felt at home.

CHAPTER THREE

Blake

Life felt better with Penny in my arms. We lay on my couch, the flames from my fireplace burning intensely, as we sipped on a light wine and cuddled. Steam billowed up from rooftops in the distance as the city lights twinkled like burning stars in the night sky. We'd gone back to how things were, the cutesy stuff, and I couldn't help but feel relieved.

Penny wrapped her arms around me and nuzzled up to my chest as my free arm wrapped around her shoulders and refused to let go. We had a white fuzzy blanket on top of us, her legs intertwined with mine, as we shared the warmth of each other's bodies.

I took a sip of my wine, swirled it around in the glass a little, and kissed her on the forehead. She looked up at me, straight in the eyes, and moved in closer for a kiss on her lips. I obliged, not even hesitating, as I felt her soft lips press against mine. A rush came over my body as I felt my face warm up. I wasn't usually like this, but with her I couldn't help it. It was as if all the things I was afraid of before didn't matter anymore. I wanted to feel like this because I knew what it meant.

"I love kissing you," she said with a smile after slowly pulling away.

"Did you miss it?" I asked.

She nodded in lieu of speaking, and I pulled her in closer and kissed her forehead again. She yawned, causing me to yawn too, before saying she was getting tired. With work for me tomorrow and school for her, I suggested getting to the bedroom and finishing our cuddling there.

Leaving the warm couch was hard but necessary. I turned off the fireplace and put our glasses on the counter for the cleaning lady to take care of tomorrow. Penny and I held hands as we walked up the large staircase towards the second floor. I'd begun to feel the slight effect of the few glasses of wine buzzing my senses, trying not to stumble as we walked upstairs.

I touched the cold metal handle to my room and a spark of static electricity ignited against my hand. The door opened and cool air pressed against my cheek as I swept Penny inside. I shut the door behind me, locking it, before turning on the bedside lamps.

"I don't have any clothes to change into," she said.

"That's never been a problem," I said with a

smile.

We walked into my bathroom before going into my closet and picking out some clothes for the both of us. We changed in front of one another and I couldn't help but feel aroused as I saw her bare skin. I reached forward, her shirt not on yet, and pulled her closer into me and nuzzled my face against hers. She smiled, her hand going onto my chest, before I kissed her softly and let her know just how much I missed her.

Penny started to breathe heavier as I kissed her neck and ran my hand down her bare goose-bumped side. I could almost smell the endorphins coursing through her body as she wrapped her arms around the back of my neck and waited for me to kiss her once again. I hesitated, though not because I didn't want to; I wanted her to beg me for my lips.

She moved in, almost without warning, and pressed her lips against mine before her tongue found its way into my mouth. I gripped her hips and pulled her closer before my hand drifted to her almost bare ass. Only a black lace thong covered her. I slapped it, gentle enough not to bruise, though hard enough to let her know I meant business. She jumped a little before I grabbed her bare ass and squeezed it firmly between my fingers. I'd missed it so much.

"I need you," she said into my ear.

"You have me," I whispered back.

"No, you don't understand. I *need* you," she whispered, as she brushed up against my growing cock.

"Then *get* some," I whispered.

Penny hopped up into my arms and I caught her. With her legs wrapped tightly around me, her arms around my neck, she kissed me passionately and sucked on my tongue like she never had before. I walked out of the closet with Penny still in my arms, took her over to the bed, and dropped her down on it. She bounced a little on the mattress as her tits jiggled a little underneath.

She spread her legs, inviting me in, before I walked forward and got down between them and propped myself up with my hands. Her hands were no strangers to my cut body as she felt me up and down, as if she were counting the number of abs I had. I nibbled on her earlobe as her head pressed into my bed.

I reached down, holding myself up with one arm, my free hand creeping up her chest, and grasped her bare breast. Her nipple hardened under my grasp as I pulled it softly. She moaned into my ear, letting me know just how much she liked me having my way with her, before my hand drifted downwards and stopped just above her panty line.

"I need it," she whispered, obviously hinting towards something a little more intense.

"Tell me what you need," I said. I wanted her to say it.

"You," she replied.

"What about me?" I asked.

"Every inch of you," she replied.

CHAPTER FOUR

Penelope

Blake touched me the way that I knew no other man ever could. His hands, while strong and passionate, were still gentle and considerate. With wine in our stomachs and any trepidation we might have had while sober gone, he ravaged my body and made me feel like a woman.

With his hand on my stomach, he bypassed my black lace panties and started to rub my clit in a circular motion as I bit my lower lip, filled with lust. I'd missed his touch so much that I knew pleasuring myself would never yield the same results as when he touched me. As his fingers became coated in my glistening juices, I reached down, his boxer briefs no match for me, pulling his cock out of his underwear and starting to stroke it.

The elastic band on his briefs pushed against the bottom of my hand as my palm ran up and down his growing shaft. I felt as he became larger and larger in my now dwarfed hand, and I knew I just wanted to taste him.

"I want to suck you," I said, his middle finger deep inside me.

"Sixty-nine?" he asked, looking me in the eyes.

I nodded, and he flipped over onto his back before slipping off his briefs and tossing them aside. I pulled off my shirt, tossed it aside, and stood up as I slid down my panties and kicked them off the bed. I twirled around, lining my pussy up with his mouth, before lowering myself down and coming face-to-face with his monstrous dick.

I felt his tongue tickle my clit as I grasped his thick shaft and licked his head like a lollipop. I saw his toes curl out of the corner of my eyes as my mouth enveloped him and I started to bob up and down. There was something primal about being in this position. It was marvelous in the best way.

Blake made me moan as his finger slid inside me and started to tap against my G-spot. I winced, though not in pain, as I felt his warm, wet tongue against me while his finger danced inside me.

"Shit," I moaned, as I jerked his cock instead of sucking it.

"I didn't say you could stop sucking," he said.

I smiled, though he couldn't see it, and gripped his balls before trying to push him as far as I could down my throat. I started to tear up as I almost choked under the immense girth of his thick dick. I knew it was never going to fit all the way down there, but I knew it turned him on a ton when I tried. Maybe it's just the effort that counts.

"I want to feel you," he said.

"You are," I replied.

"No. I want to feel *you* wrapped around *me*," he said, alluding to what I'd wanted all along.

"Have protection?" I asked.

Blake reached into his drawer and pulled out a condom before handing it to me. I ripped open the golden wrapper and pulled it out before rolling it down his wet shaft.

"How do you want me?" I asked, looking back at him.

"Just like that. I want to see that ass bouncing as I fuck you," he replied.

With my pussy starting to drip with anticipation, I leaned forward and grabbed onto his cock before rolling his head around me to get it lubed up. He grabbed my ass, holding onto it firmly, before I lowered down and slowly felt every thick inch of him push deep inside me.

I felt like I hadn't had him in so long that my pussy was almost experiencing him for the first time again. He was so big, and I felt so…*tight*. After a few times sliding up and down, though, I began to accommodate him and gripped his knees as he kept his grip firmly on my jiggling ass.

"How do you like that?" he asked.

"I love it," I said quietly.

"What?" he asked.

"I fucking love it," I said, louder.

With my knees to either side of him, I treated his cock like my own personal fuck toy and savored every inch of him. God, he was so sexy and so fucking perfect. Even a night with him without the toys was just as enjoyable, though I wouldn't mind some of them right now. Maybe another time very soon.

"Switch," he said, and I got off of him.

With me on my back, he stood next to the bed and effortlessly pulled me towards him. He grabbed my legs and put them straight up against his chest. He grabbed his cock, holding it firmly, as I looked down and watched him slide it inside me.

"Yes," I moaned.

I heard his balls clapping against my asshole as he picked up the pace from our last position and made my tits bounce faster than they ever had before. My clit, which was starting to swell, felt almost pressurized before I reached down and started to rub it. Liking that, Blake grabbed my hand and licked my fingers before sending it back down again to keep going.

He thrusted, I moaned, and I saw the sweat gleam down his body as the droplets rolled over each and every cut ab.

"Harder," I begged, grinding my teeth and gasping for air.

He obliged, picking up the pace even more, if that was even possible. I moaned each and every time his pubic bone pressed against mine. I could see the pleasure in his eyes. I knew his look more than anything, and I knew exactly what it meant.

I pulled him close to me and sucked on his lower

lip, feeling the humidity of his breath against my face. He let out a short squirm of a moan as my fingers ran through the back of his hair and his thrusts began to slow down, indicating only one thing.

"Cum for me," I whispered into his ear.

"Yes," he replied.

I went back down on the bed and extended my arms above me as he grabbed my tits and began to slow even further.

"I'm going to," he said, with a little twitch.

Blake slowed down to an almost total stop as he let out a bellow of a moan and I could feel his shaft pulsing as it pumped his load into the condom. I smiled, biting my lower lip a little in the process, as I couldn't help but feel a little more turned on any time he came inside me.

He pulled out his cock slowly and let it hang there with the condom still on before I sat up and wrapped my arms around his neck. I kissed him, slowly at first, before I put my left hand on his dripping wet chest and felt his heart racing. Even though he was finished, his tongue was no stranger to mine, and he said something that made me even more excited.

"It's your turn," he said.

"What do you mean?" I asked.

"I know you didn't get off. I *always* want you to get off with me," he said, gently pushing me down onto my back.

Getting onto his knees, he spread apart my legs and before I could make sense of what was happening, and started running his tongue all along my swollen clit. I couldn't help but moan as he used his fingers like a toy and fucked me with the middle and index as his mouth wrapped around my clit.

"Yes, just like that," I said as I looked up with tense abs and saw him looking back up at me.

His fingers were covered in my juices and I could feel myself begin to tingle. I don't know if it was the sex that led me to this point, but it felt *damn* good. With a flick of his fingers, I arched my back up high and let out a soft moan.

"Yes. I'm close," I said, but he didn't pick up the pace or slow down, instead keeping just where I wanted him to be.

With every second that passed by, I felt myself getting closer and closer as the slight tingling feeling turned into a rush of ecstasy that I couldn't ignore if I wanted to. His tongue stayed flicking my clit, his fingers deep inside me, and as if a light switch went on, it came.

"Fuck!" I screamed, as my abs tensed and my eyeballs almost rolled up into my head.

Blake didn't stop, instead amplifying my orgasm and making my skin shiver in goose-bumps. I gasped for air, the orgasm beginning to slowly fade away, as my racing heart thumped loudly. Blake's mouth left my pussy, his fingers coming out and rubbing me slowly, before he came up to my lips and kissed me softly. I could sort of taste myself, something that was still new to me, though I couldn't say I hated it.

"How was that?" he asked with a smile.

"*Amazing*," I said as beads of sweat ran down the side of my face.

"Good. I always want you to feel that way," he said.

"I feel a little sweaty. Shower?" I asked.

"Sounds like a plan," he said, grabbing my hand and helping me up.

Blake turned on his multitude of showerheads and grabbed my hand as we walked into the waterfall that waited for us. We washed each other's bodies slowly, our time between suds filled with kisses and lingering hands. After realizing we'd been in there for too long, Blake turned off the nozzles and wrapped me in a soft white towel that exuded elegance. The fibers, which were soft and fluffy, soaked up all the water that remained on my skin. Blake gave me a new shirt and shorts to wear to bed before getting some for himself.

Even though I had no makeup on, he looked at me with the same loving eyes that he did when I was all dressed up and ready for a night out. Most guys wouldn't do that, and most girls wouldn't even let a guy see them without makeup. Blake wasn't like that, though. He was a gem, and I was glad that I was lucky enough to have him.

I stretched my muscles as we got into his bed and the light sheets and comforter wrapped around my body. As I moved my feet towards his, I felt the cool, untouched area of the sheets tickle against my bare feet as Blake pulled me a little closer to him. I rested my head on his chest, listening to his heartbeat, and I couldn't help but feel completely at ease and best of all, at home.

We'd come so far from the first time I stayed

here, and even though we still had amazing sex, I could also count on moments like this that weren't normal for the man I met originally.

Blake turned off the lights and as I wrapped my arms tighter around him, his fingers started to run through my hair, playing with every strand. My eyes began to get heavy as his fingertips danced along my scalp and as they began to close fully, I heard him exhale a little, like he was giving out a sigh of relief.

To many, many more nights like this.

CHAPTER FIVE

Penelope

I looked at Blake across the table as we ate some scrambled eggs and buttermilk pancakes. I saw the way he looked at me as the rising sun beamed behind me and lit me up. I could see the lust and love in his eyes and it made me happier than I could've imagined.

"Anything exciting today?" Blake asked.

"Just the same old boring classes. It's never anything new—at least not right now," I said.

"Pretty soon you'll be done in there and won't have to ever go back. I bet you're happy about that," he said.

"I guess. There's always an unknown with it, though. It's kind of like when I graduated high school. I knew I was leaving, and I knew I was going to college and all, but there was still that unknown of how my life was going to change. I guess I'm going through that again," I said.

"I think it's that unknown that changes and helps us for the better. Sometimes things change and it can be the best thing ever," Blake said.

"Yeah, it can be," I said, smiling.

Blake definitely wasn't lying. My life changed and went in a completely different direction when we met. It was something new, something different, and it had started to turn into the best thing ever. I knew that it had even more potential for greatness.

"I've been thinking a lot about change lately. I've been thinking about the changes I want in my life, and how I want to go about getting them," Blake said.

"Go on," I said, feeling some nerves.

"I've been thinking of going home lately. *Home* home. I was thinking you could go with me," he said, taking another bite of his eggs.

I was absolutely floored when I processed his words. Did he really just ask me to go home with him? Would I meet his parents? That was the ultimate step, especially for somebody like Blake, who was incredibly private and reserved about his family and personal life. Quite honestly, I wasn't even sure how much of a family life he had, but I couldn't wait to find out.

"I'd love to. When were you thinking?" I asked.

"Well, I have some important appointments coming up, so likely not for a couple weeks or so. I know it isn't ideal, but it allows me to get them over with," he said.

"I'd probably be on spring break or close to it, then. That would be very helpful," I said.

"Then we'll mark it down. I think you'll like it," he said.

"What's it like? Where you're from," I asked.

"A fairly typical Midwestern town, I suppose. Small brick buildings with a main street that's almost crumbling under its own age and resistance to change. Empty department stores that haven't been updated or renovated in twenty years because of an overall lack of business and care. Friday night fish-fries and football games in the fall," Blake said.

"Sounds a lot like where I'm from," I said, taking a sip of water.

"Yeah, it's pretty much a painted landscape of the entire Midwest. It's nothing amazing, but it's home, even if I don't like to be there that often," he said.

"Well, thank you for letting me into your world. It means a lot to know that you trust me," I said.

He winked, grabbed his glass of orange juice, and got up from the table before taking a sip and extending his hand. He grabbed mine, pulled me in closer to him, kissed me softly, and then slapped my butt.

"Shower time before we leave?" he asked.

"Of course," I said, and he picked me up and put me over his shoulder.

I laughed as he briskly walked up the stairs with me on top of him. I couldn't help but smile, giggling like a little girl, before we entered his room and he set me down outside the shower.

Kissing me, he pulled off my clothes and turned on the water. With the warm water soon soaking our hair and bodies, the lather of his spa-like soap and shampoo trickled down our naked skin, soon washed off and running down the center drain. I cherished these moments with him even though they seemed so mundane and forgettable. There was no reason I should love simple moments like this, like a short-lived shower. But any time I was with him was extreme ecstasy that couldn't be forgotten. I needed these moments as much as I needed air.

The water soon turned off as Blake noticed the time and said we had to get moving. I had to get to class anyway, so it wasn't all bad.

"Do you need a ride to class? Gustav can take you," Blake asked.

"I need to go home first. I can't exactly go to class like this," I said, motioning up and down at my dress from last night.

"Right," he said with a laugh.

Blake called Gustav and said he'd be here in ten minutes. We wrapped things up and walked back downstairs towards the garage. I felt a bit sad, as I knew things were coming to an end for today. Blake kissed me passionately before Gustav pulled up and Blake opened my door for me and helped me inside.

"When am I seeing you again?" I asked.

"Soon. I'll call you?" he asked.

"Okay," I said, and he leaned in and gave me a peck on the lips.

The window rolled back up and Gustav drove out of the garage as Blake got into his SUV and the headlights came on. I took one last look before we drove around the corner and the sight of him was gone, but I knew it wouldn't be for long.

CHAPTER SIX

Blake

I was beginning to think that morning meetings were becoming the bane of my existence. I usually had one—a brief of sorts, to learn the movements of the company and our goals for the day. It was never anything spectacular, usually only lasting fifteen minutes or less, but it didn't make mornings any easier.

"We've seen a positive impact from the safe date protocols you asked to be put in place," Martin said.

"What were those again, exactly?" I asked.

"Tips for both men and women to keep themselves safe when they meet people from the app in person. All about danger signs, ways to verify their identity before meeting, and basic self-defense tips that could take down a potential attacker," Martin said.

"That's good. No complaints?" I asked.

"Well, of course there are some people who say we shouldn't offer anything, but we try to ignore them. Trolls, I believe the kids call them. Otherwise, everyone else seems to love them and I know the media ate it all up. Us taking a proactive stand seems to be influencing other companies to follow suit. Once again, we're trailblazers in our field," Martin said.

"Good. That will only help the stock and drive more demand for us. Nina, how are we doing with that girl who was murdered?" I asked.

"Most of the negative press has seemed to reverse as the new tips and workshop for self-defense is lightening everyone up. People are shifting their focus back onto us, and in a good way," Nina said.

"Great. Is there anything else we need to discuss today?" I asked as I looked around the room.

Nobody raised their hand or said a word, instead shaking their heads no, before I thanked them for the updates and left the room to get back to my office, where I knew I had a heaping pile of papers and files to sort through today. The work never seemed to stop, no matter how badly I wanted it to.

"Good morning, Mr. Hunter, sir," Grace said as I walked up to her desk.

"Good morning, Grace," I said, opening my door.

"Your mother called for you. Would you like me to patch her through?" Grace asked.

"No, thank you, though. I'll handle it," I said

before entering my office.

I didn't have much contact with my mother. It wasn't that things were bad between us, but I just never felt incredibly close to her or my father. I took care of everyone in my family, the older and disabled ones, anyway, but I didn't receive the warmth and love as a child that I felt I needed. Maybe that was why I'd turned into the person I was before I met Penny. Maybe my childhood explained a lot about me and the man I became.

I took out my cell phone and loaded my contacts before coming across my mom's entry and clicking it to dial. It connected and the phone began to ring as I stood in front of my windows, my left hand in my pocket as my right hand firmly held the phone.

"Hello?" my mother asked.

"Hello, Mom," I said.

"Oh, Blake, honey! I'm so glad you could call me back," she said in an overtly ecstatic voice.

"Of course, Mom. How are things? Do you need something?" I asked.

"Oh, no, things are good. I'm being well taken care of here. I just wanted to talk to you. I miss your voice. I saw you in the newspaper, you know," she said.

"I miss your voice as well. What was I in there for?" I asked.

"That, what do you call it, self-defense thing you have going on for the ladies. Oh, it's so nice. I'm so happy you thought of that to help those women," she said.

"It's my pleasure, Mom. I like giving back and

helping out," I said, clearing my throat.

Talks with my mother were never exciting, but I thought they were for her. Part of me wanted to believe that she felt guilty about the way things were and had been over the years and she was trying to change that before the time came when she no longer could. I didn't blame her for being a bad mother, and I'd gotten over it, but I didn't think she had or ever would. I think she still wanted to believe that there was some ray of hope for us. I lost that shred of hope a long time ago, and I wasn't sure there was a way to regain it.

"Talking about ladies, do you have a lady in your life? I'd love to get grandchildren before I croak," she said in jest.

"Well, I can't promise you grandchildren, but yes, I am seeing someone," I said.

"That's wonderful, dear! What's her name?" she asked.

I could hear the enthusiasm and excitement in her voice. I never *saw* anybody, at least not officially, except for *her*, the last woman, the woman who changed everything. That was so long ago that I think my mother was starting to wonder if I'd ever be with someone again. I guess I had to show her things were okay.

"Her name is Penelope. She's a nice girl. I think you could meet her soon. If you want to, that is," I said.

"Of course! Your father and I would just love to meet her. Are you bringing her by?" she asked.

"Eventually, yes. Maybe in a few weeks? We both

have some work to square away, but I'm fairly positive we'll be coming out," I said.

"You just made my entire year, you know that? I wish you could see me. I'm absolutely beaming," she said.

"Me too, Mom," I said as I looked down.

"Blake, honey, your aunt Karen is calling. Is it okay if I let you go?" my mother asked.

"Yes, I'll talk to you later," I said.

"Goodbye. I love you," she said.

"You too, Mom," I said before hanging up.

I set my phone down and took a deep breath before holding it in for a few seconds and exhaling slowly. Why was this so damn difficult? Why couldn't I be like the scores of other people who had a relationship with their parents? A real one, not the one I had. Sure, I had it better than some people who had no relationship with their parents whatsoever, if they even knew their parents, but I wanted it to be better. I guess at my age it was pretty much a pipe dream. I was lucky to have living parents, as I knew some of my peers didn't.

Left with only my thoughts, I sorted through my work for the day and made a few business calls. The morning was early, far too early, though I suppose business never really sleeps.

A few hours later, closer to lunch, I received a special text that made my mood a little bit better.

"*I miss you,*" it read.

So simple, that text, yet so powerful, even though it was only three words. Penny had a way of doing that, of taking my mind off other things, even if she wasn't trying to. I could depend on that sanity at just the right moments, as if she were sitting behind me and watching what I was doing, just waiting until the perfect moment to give me her encouraging words.

I really was lucky to have her in my life again. I knew it would be the last time we'd ever have to go through a situation like we had twice before, and I hoped that meant we weren't going to spilt apart again. It was so grueling, breaking up, and I thought it affected me just as much as it did her. Hell, maybe it hurt me a little bit more than it hurt her. I'd gotten so attached, at least as much as I could.

I reciprocated her message, telling her I missed her even more, to which she replied that it wasn't possible. She missed me way more than I missed her, and as I wrote out and sent my rebuttal on why I missed her more, it hit me. We were becoming a couple. A *real* couple. Not just one who were together, but one who dreamt of being together. The cutesy type of couple I'd never really been, even before, though I guess I was okay with it.

I'd never really thought about it much before, being that type of guy in that kind of relationship, but I couldn't say that it was horrible. It was, for lack of a better word, nice.

Grace brought in my lunch, a California club with extra bacon, a side salad, and baked chips as I took out a bottle of water from the small fridge in my office. I told her to take an extended lunch if she wanted, an extra half-hour, to which she seemed very happy and grateful. That girl worked a ton and did a good job, so I thought she deserved an extra break.

I sat and texted Penny while I leisurely ate my lunch and flipped through the news on my computer. The markets were up in Asia, which was nice considering I had many investments there. I did a search for the company and myself, coming up with a bunch of articles corresponding to the stuff I was told in my meetings earlier today, which was always a good sign. I didn't think my staff expected me to search these things, so it was nice to know that they weren't lying to me and telling me what I wanted to hear while secretly dealing with crises.

As I finished my lunch and wiped off my hands, I texted Penny and let her know that I was going to be out of commission for a few hours while I worked. She said okay, and sent me some kissy faces. I locked my phone, a smile on my face, and got back to work.

That girl was something else, that was for sure.

CHAPTER SEVEN

Penelope

"I fucking hate the prick," Nicolette exclaimed as she walked through our apartment door and slammed it behind her.

"What happened?" I asked, in shock. I was damn glad I wasn't that guy.

"I went out with Mike, the so called '*good guy*,' and he led me on before telling me that he thought we should see other people," she said.

"What? Why? You two were doing good," I said.

"He said he wanted to explore other options and not be tied down to just one girl. What a load of shit. He told me the complete opposite a week ago. I think he just met some stupid slut who spread her legs full eagle. Whatever. I don't need him," she said, grabbing a beer from the fridge and walking over towards me.

She sat on the couch beside me, curled up, and put her head on my shoulder as the glow from the television screen illuminated us in the otherwise fairly dark room. I felt a little bad for her, knowing what I had and she craved, though I guess in a way it was her own fault. After all, she did just talk to any guy who was attractive enough and would give her the time of day, even though she knew nothing about them and had nothing in common with them. It was like she was so happy just to have somebody into her that she'd toss everything else aside to get that attention. I hated it and I hated seeing her like this.

"Well, I just want you to know that any guy would be lucky to have you. You're a great girl and I know you have a lot to offer somebody," I said.

"Yeah, right. If that were the case, guys would be dying to see me and date me," she said.

I could tell she was annoyed, pissed, and hurt, so I knew not to rock the boat and start any kind of argument with her. She was a hardheaded woman anyway, so it was best not to keep pushing in her face how good and great she was. She wouldn't believe it anyway, at least not right now.

"You just haven't found the right guy. He'll come, I know it," I said.

"I hope. I'm not sure how many more losers I can go through before that time comes, though. You're lucky—having Blake, and having that kind of love I can only dream of. Hopefully my billionaire prince comes soon. Oh, maybe he'll be a *real* prince. Yeah, I'd like that," she said, perking up a little.

"Me too, Nicolette. Me too," I said.

I awoke to knocking on the front door as Nicolette was getting ready for work.

"Who could that be?" she asked as she walked over and looked out the peephole.

She unlocked and opened the door to the grocery delivery guys standing there with bags of groceries at their feet.

"I didn't hear you buzz," Nicolette said in a confused voice.

"An older woman was leaving and let us in. If you could please sign this, I'd greatly appreciate it," the man said.

"Here," I said, walking over and signing their sheet.

"Would you like us to bring the bags inside?" the guy asked.

"No, thank you, we have it," I said with a friendly smile.

"Okay, have a good day!" the man said, and they turned around and left.

"One good thing about you dating Blake is this. I love free food," Nicolette said as she grabbed two of the canvas bags and brought them into the kitchen.

I grabbed the other two and locked the door behind me before putting my bags down and starting to unload them. I'd forgotten all about Blake sending us some more food. He'd told me through text last night that he was ordering some, but I couldn't believe it came already.

"Blake doesn't have any friends, does he?" Nicolette asked from the bathroom.

"Of course he has friends," I said.

"No, I mean friends who are single. You know. *Friends*," she said, sticking her head out the doorway.

"Oh, I'm not sure about that. I guess I can bring it up to him sometime if you want," I said.

"Please and thank you. Maybe I'm not the problem, but just where I've been looking. I need to up my game a little bit," she said before turning on the blow dryer.

Blake, being big on whole foods and not eating things that were too processed, had sent me many of the same things he liked to eat, which wasn't horrible, but it wasn't exactly my taste, either. I didn't mind chips, sugary snacks, and toaster pastries. In fact, I kind of liked them. I knew it wasn't the healthiest diet, but I wasn't trying to get on the front of any fitness magazines anytime soon. All Blake sent me were fruits, vegetables, and premade meals that looked so healthy I knew they wouldn't have the same taste as my normal fare.

After putting away my food, I looked at the clock and whispered an obscenity before running into my room and changing my clothes. My hair looked greasy and unkempt, a result of a third day not washing it, calling for a quick spray of dry shampoo and a ponytail to look somewhat presentable for class.

I grabbed my notebook, books, and phone before stuffing them all in my bag and telling Nicolette goodbye for the day. I couldn't believe I'd slept in that long. I'd swear my alarms never went off.

I sped down the stairs like a madwoman before running outside to the bus stop. It was just pulling away as I waved my arms and through some kind of miracle, it stopped and the doors opened. I'd never been so lucky. I found a seat, the last one available, and caught my breath before checking my phone and e-mail. Six spam messages, mostly about clothing sales. I deleted all of them even though I desperately wanted to look through them and gaze at what I couldn't have.

The bus let off and I ran out the doors and past the other riders before getting inside the building and seeing I had about five minutes until my class started. Walking slower, though still a little quickly, I went up a few flights of stairs and got into my class with barely any time to spare. I sat down in an open seat, unpacked my books, and caught my breath as the professor started writing on the whiteboard.

The lesson, which was about operative conditioning, was rather interesting, even if my professor didn't do the best job conveying that. It started to make me wonder if I could ever fall for something like that. I'd like to think I was too smart to be conditioned, but then again I was sure all the subjects thought the same thing when they were experimented on. They were probably just as cocky as I was right now, and that was their downfall.

My focus naturally shifted to whether I could

condition another person, or if they'd see right through my games. I wasn't the best liar, and in a way conditioning kind of felt like lying, even if it wasn't exactly like it. I'd be withholding information from them and bending their will, in a sense. Maybe it was best to let the professionals deal with this.

My hand started to cramp as I scribbled down my notes as fast as I could. A few other people in class used their laptops to type notes, which made me wonder if I should start bringing my laptop to my classes. It seemed a bit sad I only thought of it now, a few months before graduation, instead of when I first got here, but I supposed there was nothing I could do about that now.

I took a few breaks from writing, hoping my memory would be strong enough to remember everything my professor was saying, even though I knew some of the information would likely fall through the cracks. It always did.

After taking three pages of notes and trying to remember the rest, the class was over and I could breathe a short sigh of relief and ice my hand in preparation for the next time I needed to write like this.

"And don't forget to start on your papers for the end of the semester. I know it's a bit away, but I need to approve your topic before you can start. Failure to get my written permission will result in an automatic failure for the assignment. It's also forty percent of your grade, so there will be no way to pass without getting it done. Have a good rest of your day."

My final semester in school and of course I had

some massive paper to get done. It seemed only fitting that it'd happen to me. Maybe Blake could help me think of a topic. He was smart.

Speaking of Blake, I had a date with him later tonight at his place, and I couldn't wait. He'd invited over two friends, another couple, to join us so that we could double. Being included in his world and meeting his friends was enough proof for me that things were moving in the right direction. A guy, especially one like Blake, wouldn't bring his friends over to meet me if he didn't see *something* with me. I knew that we were going forward, and the things we did to one another before were behind us.

After sitting through a quiz and another lecture, I took the bus home, went up to the apartment, and pulled a pineapple-mango smoothie that Blake had sent over from the fridge. I took a few sips, puckered at how tart it was, and put it back before I sucked my cheeks. I didn't know how he ate this healthy stuff.

"Are you nervous? What if they're pricks?" Nicolette asked as I got ready.

"They won't be. Blake likes them a lot and only had nice things to say about them," I said.

"Yeah, because they're in *his* world. They're likely rich themselves, and they probably only hang around other people of their status. You aren't that, far from it, actually. I'm just afraid that you won't have anything in common with them," Nicolette said.

"I don't have to have a lot in common with them. It isn't as if we're all going to become best friends. It's just a nice dinner with another couple. It's something you do when you're with someone. I probably won't ever see them again outside of another dinner date," I said.

"Whatever you say. Just remember to act snooty and rich. I bet they'll respond well," she said.

I rolled my eyes and finished curling my hair before spraying myself with some rose perfume and going to get my shoes and bag. Gustav was set to be here within ten minutes, per his text, and I wanted to make sure I didn't keep him waiting. I just wanted to make sure I got to Blake's place before the other two got there. It'd be a little awkward to be the last person there.

"Okay, I better get going," I said as I grabbed my coat and slipped it on.

I felt so boring wearing the same black dress over and over, but I didn't really have much else to wear, at least in a social situation like this. Blake said it wouldn't be super casual and to wear a dress, so this was all I could really do. Maybe I should see if he'd buy me a new one so that I didn't always look the same. I was sure someone someday would notice I always wore the same dress to his date nights and events.

"Be good and don't forget to act snooty. Don't let them walk all over you," Nicolette said as she rummaged through the fridge.

"I'll try not to," I said, walking out the door.

Gustav, who was just pulling up as I walked out

of the building, got out and opened my door for me before helping me down into the backseat. With my purse firmly in my lap, he got back into the driver's seat and adjusted his mirror.

"Ready for tonight?" he asked.

"I guess. I'm not sure how to prepare for something like this. I don't know anything about these people," I said.

"I had an interaction with them once. I picked them up for Mr. Hunter about a year ago. They're nice people, for what it's worth. I'm sure you'll have a good evening with them," Gustav said.

"That's reassuring. Thank you," I said.

He pulled out onto the street as I looked out the window at the night sky above. The air had been warming up a little as the days passed, though it still felt far from spring. I couldn't wait until the summer, and for more reasons than one.

As Gustav pulled into Blake's building, I felt my stomach gurgle a little as the butterflies fluttered and I tried to keep my nerves in check.

"You'll be fine," Gustav said, looking back at me.

"Yeah, I hope so," I replied.

CHAPTER EIGHT

Blake

I patiently awaited the arrival of my love as my garage door buzzed and I walked over to the elevator. I saw Penny on the small screen and let her up as I waited next to the door for her beautiful face to greet me.

My friends, Brian and Maggie Jameson, hadn't yet arrived, though I knew they'd be here shortly. Everything was set, including the food, which was finishing up cooking. I had wine out, appetizers sitting on the counter, and a small fire roaring nearby. Everything was perfect, and would be even more so once those doors opened and I saw her face light up.

"I missed you," she said with gusto.

"And I missed you," I said before we embraced and her perfume tickled my senses.

She leaned back a little, though still in my arms,

and smiled, and I leaned forward and pressed my lips against hers. I could taste her peach lip balm as it made my taste buds awaken and come on full alert. This was always a highlight to my day.

"Are your friends here yet?" she asked.

"No, not yet," I said, with my arms still clasped around her.

"Good. I was nervous that I was going to get here late. I wanted to be here to greet them with you," she said.

"Understandable. You don't know them, so I'd assume you'd feel awkward getting here last. I will say that they're very down to earth and you have nothing to worry about. They're actually fun to be around, especially compared to some other couples I could've chosen for tonight," I said.

Just as I'd finished speaking, a buzz came from my intercom. I let go of Penny and walked across the room towards my front door, which I very rarely used, except for guests. I saw them in the video feed standing outside and buzzed them in, before buzzing again once they were in the vestibule, which was a feature added for security purposes. There were a lot of high net-worth individuals in this building, and they wanted to make sure that we were fully protected and that nobody could slip inside easily. Even the windows in the building were bulletproof.

"I'm nervous," Penny said as she came up to me and grabbed my hand.

"Don't be. I'm here with you all the way," I said in a comforting tone.

Within a minute there was a knock at the door. I

looked at Penny and saw the anxiety in her eyes. I wished I could take it away and make her feel at ease, but I knew that meeting new people wasn't always her thing, especially when she believed that they were going to judge her or make her feel unwelcome. Brian and Maggie were far from that, though, and they used to be poor before building their clothing company, so if any of my friends are going to be kind to Penny, it was them.

I opened the door and was met with two smiling faces as we said our hellos and they came inside. Penny stood there, looking a bit shy, like she thought she should say something but she didn't know what exactly to say.

"Brian, Maggie, this is Penny. Penny, this is Brian and Maggie Jameson," I said.

"Hello, it's so nice to meet you. We've heard a lot," Brian said, and he and Maggie shook Penny's hand.

"Likewise," she said, even though I knew she was lying and just being polite.

"Please, take your coats off and be at home," I said, taking their coats and hanging them up.

"It smells wonderful in here," Maggie said as the four of us walked towards the kitchen.

"I'd hope so. I sourced only the best meal for the four of us tonight. Also, would any of you like a drink? I have a beautiful wine for the evening, if you're interested. I also have every other drink imaginable," I said with a smile.

"I'll take a glass of your wine," Maggie said.

"Same for me," Brian said.

"Yes, please," Penny said.

"So, Penny, I hear you're a college student?" Maggie asked as I walked over towards the wine.

"Yes, I'm in my last semester, so I'm hoping to land a job in my field soon," Penny said.

"What field?" Maggie asked.

"Computer science," Penny replied.

"Wow, that's amazing. I love that you're in that field. There certainly aren't enough women in STEM fields. How is it?" Maggie asked as she sat down at the counter and looked at Penny intently.

"Well, it's something I've always loved," Penny said, sitting down across from her. "I guess it's hard sometimes, not because of the workload or anything, but because of the stigma and my colleagues. It's very testosterone-driven, if you know what I mean."

"Ugh, tell me about it. I can't remember a job I've had where the females outnumbered the men. Even now there are a ton of men at our company. We really need to fix that," Maggie said as she looked at Brian.

"Blake said you own a clothing company?" Penny asked.

"Yes, we do. Mostly urban chic apparel for all ages. We try to make affordable clothing that's accessible and fashionable. It's a challenge, but somehow we've made it happen," Maggie said.

I looked at Penny with loving eyes as she hit it off with Maggie and was pulled into the conversation. There was something warming about seeing her engulfed in my world and thriving. It was like another nail in the argument for being with her, and it only made me like her even more. As I poured the wine and handed out the glasses, she looked at me, her eyes looking happy and calm, as if the stresses and anxiety from earlier had totally left her body and she was at ease.

I was proud of her.

CHAPTER NINE

Penelope

It's amazing how insecure we can sometimes become in life. Here I was, completely afraid that things were going to go poorly this evening, and it turned out to be a more wonderful time than I could have imagined. Maggie and Brian were both nice to me, neither one of them ever talking down to me or acting like I wasn't there. I don't know why I was worried before that I'd be ignored, but I think it stemmed from me worrying that I was just going to be some kid to them.

While Blake wasn't too much older than me, I was still only in my early twenties. They were in their early thirties, and it made me wonder if they looked at hanging out with me like me hanging out with an early teenager. We were from two almost different generations, and the divide might be too great to form any strong conversations that would bring us together.

I was glad I was wrong about that, though, and that things actually were amazing. Our meal, which was roasted chicken with some kind of brown-sugar-like glaze, melted in my mouth and the subtle bitterness of the wine complemented it beautifully. Our conversation wasn't even focused too much on business or stocks, but rather on normal topics, including sports and movies. Maggie mostly talked to me the entire time as the guys talked hockey and kept to themselves, and I learned all about what it was like to own a clothing business.

She even said that she'd give my information to her human resources people for after I graduated because she knew I was a strong woman with a great work ethic and that I knew my stuff. Before, I didn't want Blake to help me too much with finding a job, because I didn't want to seem needy or dependent on him, but I was now a bit more open to the proposition, especially because of how it came to be. He didn't make any calls for me; instead, I used my own charisma and personality to make an impression on an employer who saw the potential in me that I only dreamed one would see.

Not only that, but I thought that I could do well working for a clothing company—especially one that made somewhat fashionable and chic clothing. Nicolette was always bitching that I needed to update my wardrobe, and I was sure that I'd get some kind of discount on the company's items. I'd hope so, anyway.

After a final glass of wine, Blake asked if we'd like coffee and dessert. Looking at one another, Maggie and Brian both agreed, even though it was starting to get a little late. I was a bit tired, but didn't say anything or excuse myself because of how wonderful the conversation had gotten. I didn't hang out with people that often, at least nobody other than Nicolette, and it was refreshing to meet new people and have different experiences. They brought me into a world that I hadn't quite known existed before.

"I've seen news about a merger in the papers recently, Blake. How's that going?" Brian asked after Blake brought over the coffee and cake.

"It's going, though it's all a bit stressful. I didn't know that acquiring them would be such a nuisance. The current owners all want a little too much in terms of both power and money. I'm not sure we're willing to give them everything they want. Sometimes you just have to draw a line and stand behind it," Blake said.

"Agreed. At least you're in that position, though. I think the other owners know that they're getting a great deal and that your company can take theirs further than they ever could on their own. Sometimes it's worth it to see your company go further and help even more people than it did before. They'll come around, I'm sure of it," Brian said.

"When we acquired that small lingerie line last spring, we weren't sure how it would pan out. Of course, it wasn't anywhere near as large as your company or your deal, but we eventually worked it out. I say just give them eighty percent of what they want and call it a day. We did, and now the lines we bought are selling like you wouldn't believe. Sometimes something proprietary, in our case the designs on the bras themselves, is worth more than what you give the other people," Maggie said.

"Penny, what do you think? You're awful quiet over there," Blake said as he looked at me from across the aisle.

Me? What did I know? I knew nothing about business or mergers or any of that stuff. I was just a computer science student who was happiest sitting in her little room coding and working by herself.

"Oh, I don't know," I said with a nervous smile.

"Nonsense. I know you're one of the smartest women I've ever known, and I greatly value your input. What should I do in this situation?" Blake asked.

"Well, I agree with Maggie. Give them what they want within reason and reap the benefits of what they have to give you. It's better to spend a little more money now, and get a lot more back later. Besides, every day you spend in negotiations without their product or service is another day of earnings lost in the long run," I said, tightly gripping my cup of coffee in my hands.

"I've never thought of it that way. You're right, we're losing money every single day we stay in negotiations with them. The faster we get out, the faster we can implement their stuff and make money. We're only losing money until then," Blake said.

"So, what are you going to do?" Brian asked.

"Give them most of what they want. The board will just have to deal with it," Blake said, whipping out his phone and firing off a quick e-mail.

"Great job, Penny," Maggie said with a smile.

Looking at me from across the table, Blake winked before taking a sip of his coffee. I felt a warm feeling in my stomach, almost like a job well done, before I took another sip and finished the rest of my cup.

After about fifteen minutes, Maggie and Brian got up and said they better get going so they could get home to the sitter. Blake and I walked them over to the front door, helped them with their belongings, and said our goodbyes.

"I'm serious about giving your information to the right people at the company," Maggie said, giving me her card. "Get me your resume and I'll give you a personal recommendation for our web division."

"Thank you so much for the opportunity and the kind words tonight. I'll be sure to get you the information and the files," I said.

She gave me a big hug, as did Brian, and as they walked out of the front door and back towards the elevator, I couldn't help but stand there with a small smile on my face. Did I really just do all of that? Did I go from the shy girl who was almost sweating because of them coming over, to just about landing a job upon graduation? I didn't know how I pulled it off, but it appeared that I somehow did.

Blake shut the door and grabbed me, pulling me in and giving me a soft kiss on the lips. I breathed in quickly and hard through my nose, my eyes shut, as he took me completely by surprise.

"What was that for?" I asked after our lips left one another's.

"Thank you for being so amazing tonight," he said, kissing me on the cheek.

"It's no problem at all. I really liked them. They were nice," I said.

"See, I told you, but you were still worried for whatever reason. Hopefully we can do this more often," Blake said before walking over and taking care of the dishes on the table.

This dinner going so well tonight also made me feel a bit more secure about my future with Blake, in a weird way. I felt like tonight going so well only reaffirmed for him that he could trust me and keep me around. He could feel that I wouldn't embarrass him or make him look like an idiot around friends and important business colleagues. I would only lift him up and make him look as great as he was. That was job security, though in this case more in the relationship sense.

"Getting tired?" he asked as he looked at the clock.

"Very," I said as I stretched and yawned.

"Sorry it went so long. We can go get in bed now," he said, turning off the kitchen lights.

Holding hands, we walked upstairs towards his bedroom. The nightstand lamps turned on and his crisp white sheets were cool to the touch as I jumped on them and lay back. Smiling, he changed clothes before I got up and did the same.

With my things still there, I took out my face

wash and toothbrush and finished getting ready for bed, and all the while Blake stood behind me, his hands on my hips, his presence was enough to send chills up and down my spine. As I turned around, my teeth freshly brushed and minty, he kissed me, though not passionately. I almost had to stand on my tippy toes just to reach his lips.

Holding my hand, he guided me to the bed, where we quickly both got in and snuggled up under the covers.

"Turn over," he said, motioning for me to flip.

I obliged, flipping onto my side, before I felt him come up behind me and wrap his arms around me. Being the little spoon, I curled up a little as I grabbed his hand and brought it to my mouth. I kissed it, held it tight, and refused to let it go as I felt the warmth of his body against mine.

Safe and enveloped in the ecstasy of his body, I soon fell asleep, my eyes no longer able to hold themselves open, even though I wanted nothing more than to look into his eyes for just a little bit longer. Oh well, maybe I could in my dreams.

"Wake up, sleepy," I heard as my eyes struggled to open.

The glare of the sun beamed into my eyes as I moaned a little and held up my forearm to block it. Blake was sitting on the edge of the bed with coffee in his hand.

"What time is it?" I asked.

"Just past seven. I made you some coffee," he said.

I sat up, my eyes still a little closed, before I grabbed the coffee and brought it up to my lips. The aroma of the roasted beans mixed in with a little cream wafted into my nose, and I could taste the exquisite brew before I'd even sipped it.

The coffee tingled against my tongue as I took my first sip while Blake brushed my hair back with his fingers. His morning stubble defined his jaw and his somewhat messy hair was a welcome sight for a man who always liked to look perfect.

He leaned forward and kissed my forehead before getting up and walking into his closet.

"How do you like this today?" he asked as he held up a suit and tie.

"It looks perfect," I said, and he hung it up.

"So, I forgot to mention it to you earlier, but I talked to my mother about us visiting soon," Blake said.

"Oh?" I asked, intrigued.

"She said she couldn't wait to meet you. She's very excited," he said.

"That's great. I'm sure we're going to have a great time," I said, a sense of relief echoing throughout my body.

"You still want to come, right?" he asked, peeking his head out of the doorway and looking at me.

"Of course, if you want me to, that is. I'd understand if you wanted to go alone," I said.

"No, not at all. I just want you to know that the place isn't exactly amazing. There isn't much of anything to do," he said.

"Hey, I'm from a small Midwestern town too, remember? I know exactly how much and how little there is to do in them," I said.

"Yeah, I guess you're right. I just wanted to make sure you were prepared. Your break is coming up soon, correct?" he asked.

"Very soon. I think it's two weeks from this Friday, actually, but I could always leave on Friday if you wanted," I said.

"I'll have Grace make travel arrangements later today," Blake said.

"Where will we be staying?" I asked.

"With them. There's exactly one motel in the area, and it's not the kind of place you'd want to stay in. That is, unless you want to sleep on bedbugs and tear-soaked mattresses," he said with a smirk.

"You're horrible," I said, setting down my coffee and walking towards him.

I gave him a soft kiss before changing my clothes and pulling back my hair. My classes were a little bit later today, so I figured I'd just shower at home since he seemed to be already bathed and cleaned up. No point in standing inside that huge shower all by myself.

I went downstairs with my coffee and had some

fresh fruit and toast before Blake, fixing his tie as he walked, came down the stairs and quickly ate some himself.

"I can drive you home if you want," he said.

"I'd love that," I replied with my coffee at my lips.

CHAPTER TEN

Blake

I grabbed my keys and belongings as Penny picked up her purse and phone from the table. It was always sad when we had to leave one another, but I held onto the joy of knowing I'd see her again soon. I guess absence does make the heart grow fonder.

Holding hands, we took the elevator down to the garage and I helped her into the front seat of the SUV before closing her door and walking around to my side. I saw my neighbor, the one who lived below me, getting into his car, and I gave a friendly wave and he reciprocated. I wasn't too close with my neighbors, though I suppose we were all friendly towards one another. It was kind of sad considering where I came from. Everyone back home was always coming over and pushing themselves into your business. In fact, there was no such thing as just *your* business. Everyone knew everything about everyone, and everyone gave their opinions. Not so much here.

The massive, hulking garage door opened and we slowly drove out onto the street as the traffic had just begun to accumulate for the day. I didn't live right on an insanely busy street, but I suppose at morning rush hour every street in San Francisco is busy and hellish.

With only my left hand on the top of the wheel, Penny held my right hand while she flipped through her phone. As we sat at a light not too far from her apartment, I looked over at her slyly and watched her. She was completely oblivious. She was so beautiful, so perfect, and I only wished I could spend all my time with her. She helped me, and in many more ways than one.

As if the ride were only minutes long, we soon pulled up in front of her apartment and I knew that our time together, at least for now, had come to a close. She looked at me with saddened eyes, our fingers still laced together as if they'd never come untied.

"When will I see you again?" she asked.

"Soon," I replied, without giving her an exact answer.

"It better be. I'm going to miss you," she said with love in her eyes.

"And I you, beautiful girl," I replied.

Leaning in, she gave me a soft kiss on the lips, and I felt the endorphins rush through my body, making me feel calm and at ease. I could still taste the soft hints of coffee upon her lips as it lingered on mine, even after her lips departed.

I licked them, tasting her, as she smiled and let go of my hand before grabbing her purse from the floor and dropping her phone inside.

"Text me later," she said, putting her fingers on the handle.

"Count on it," I said, giving her another quick peck on the lips.

Smiling, she opened the door and got out of the car before walking up to her door. I watched her to make sure she got in okay until she closed the door behind her and waved to me before blowing me a kiss. I showed a small smile, winked at her, and pulled off the curb, beginning the commute to my office. Within minutes, I caught myself looking at the passenger seat in hopes that she'd somehow still be there, and I wouldn't have just had to drop her off. Sadly, though, she was gone, and I was now alone and missing her.

There was a small crowd around the building as I pulled into the parking garage.

"What's this all about?" I asked Steven, one of the security guards.

"Some pop star is nearby, I believe. I think some other company in the building is talking to her," Steven said.

Shaking my head, I rolled my window back up and pulled into my parking space. This happened every now and again, with some famous person or another inside the building working on their next big business deal that would net them millions in royalties and fees. We had someone once but didn't pen a deal, as after more thought we began to think that they wouldn't bring much to the table. After all, we were dealing with a dating app, not something more tangible.

I got out of the car, grabbed my bag from the backseat, and walked towards my private elevator before scanning my key and saying hello to the guards outside. Looking at my watch, I timed the ride up, which happened to take exactly thirty-three seconds. The doors opened and Grace, who was alerted to me arriving, was standing outside with some folders in her hands.

"Good morning, Grace," I said as I stepped out of the elevator.

"Good morning, Mr. Hunter. Here are your files for the meeting. Everyone is waiting for you," she said.

"Do me a favor," I said as she walked beside me.

"Yes sir, what is it?" she asked.

"Book travel arrangements for two weeks from this Friday. I'm taking Penny to my home for a few days, so we'll need flights and car transport for two," I said.

"Certainly. Is there anything else you need help with?" she asked as we approached the conference room door.

"No, that will be it, thank you," I said before entering.

"There he is," I heard as I walked inside.

As I looked in the room, I saw a few new faces that I hadn't seen before. One was Carmen Kincaid, a rather famous woman who I hadn't met. She did a lot of television work, some movies, and was everywhere in the media. This must be who everybody was waiting for outside.

"Good morning, all. What's on the docket for today?" I asked.

"We have Ms. Kincaid here, as you can see. She came to us today with a proposition for a sponsorship deal," Martin said.

"Oh?" I asked.

"Ms. Kincaid would like to find love, Mr. Hunter. Obviously, finding it can be hard, as she doesn't want to date someone in the business. We thought, what better way than to put her in the app? She can selectively find and choose people, and it would be great press for us," Martin said.

"How so?" I asked, crossing my legs.

"Let me take it from here," a man said, who was seated next to Carmen. "Mr. Hunter, my name is Leon, and I'm Ms. Kincaid's manager. What we're thinking is using the app to present an opportunity. Carmen can search for love, we make it a public affair, and the world gets to see her use your app."

"It would bring a lot of people onto the app who either have never been on, or who haven't been on in a while," Martin said.

"All those men, and likely some women, will be creating accounts and logging in to see her profile. They'll want to be matched with her, and hopefully, go out with her. It will lead to a lot of positive press, Ms. Kincaid will go on dates with some of these men, and talk about how great the app is and how easy it is to use. With this endorsement, other celebrities might follow. It's a win-win for everybody involved," Leon said.

I sat there stroking my chin as I looked off and thought about the proposition. It wasn't a particularly bad idea, not in any sense, but it did make me a little nervous. While I was all for furthering the company and our message, was this the way I wanted to do it? By having a celebrity endorsing it, and not genuinely or organically at that?

What if it all looked fake to the media and general public? That was a huge risk, and one that could hurt our, and my, reputation. On the other hand, it would bring us even further into the public eye and possibly cement us as *the* dating app and service to use. Nobody else was getting the endorsement of a mega-celebrity.

"I can see the value you and your client are offering to our company. After all, nobody else is doing this. I am open to the idea, but it needs to be done in the correct way. It can't seem forced or fake. The public needs to think that you wanted this yourself, to actually find someone, and not that we approached you for some kind of publicity stunt. That will only hurt both parties," I said.

"We feel the exact same way. While Carmen is looking for love and that person to spend her time with, she also sees the value in promoting this from a business perspective. We can guarantee you, to your face, that this is a wholesome and truthful endeavor," Leon said.

"Then we can move forward and get it done. We'll mount a marketing campaign, including advertising inside the app once her profile is up and everything is secure. We'll make sure you have privileges that normal members don't have," I said.

"Thank you so much, Mr. Hunter. I greatly appreciate it," Carmen said.

"Please, call me Blake. Is there any other business?" I asked, as I looked around the room.

With nobody saying yes or bringing anything up, I grabbed my folders from the lacquered wood table and left for my office, where Grace was sitting outside.

"I have your plans all set, Mr. Hunter. Would you like me to send you the itinerary?" Grace asked.

"Yes, thank you," I said with a smile before going into my office and setting the folders down on my desk.

It looked like it was all set. Now to hope that nothing happened between now and then.

CHAPTER ELEVEN

Penelope

A few days had passed since I'd last seen Blake. We'd both been busy, with me gearing up for midterms and studying my ass off to keep good grades while Blake worked on work stuff, obviously, which I never understood or even tried to understand.

We'd made plans for tonight to meet for dinner and then go back to his place, which I was very excited about. I'd missed everything about him: his scent, his touch, the way he wrapped his arms around me, and the very essence of him. He was like the drug I needed to take and I was going through withdrawal without him.

I sat in my room later that day working on an app project I'd been working on since I started college. It wasn't anything special, just a game, but I loved tinkering around with it when things got boring. I guess it was just a good stress-reliever when I needed to unwind and take things slow.

The game involved a series of planks that you would just jump between and try to get a high score. Your guy would be running endlessly, and you'd tap to jump while also trying to avoid traps in place to slow you down and take away your health. I'd greatly improved the graphics over time, even bartering services with an artist friend I had my sophomore year, but I'd never published it or even thought about doing anything with it. I guess I didn't care about the money so much, but just the experience and knowledge of making something and seeing it come to life. I'd done all this myself, aside from the little bit of art in the game, and I loved knowing that I was capable. It was an empowering feeling.

After about an hour working on the app and refining it further, I felt my eyes start to get dry, as I'd been staring at the computer screen for far too long without rest. I saved the game, closed my laptop, and grabbed one of my textbooks, my communications one, before sitting up against my headboard and opening it to my required reading chapter.

As I got further into reading, though, the words began to blend together as I struggled to keep my eyes open long enough to comprehend what I was reading. Acting quickly, I set an alarm on my phone for two hours from now, which was when I needed to get ready for my date, before putting my head back against my pillow and letting nature take its course. Besides, I needed my rest for tonight—at least I hoped I'd need a lot of energy.

"I hate this thing," I said as I struggled to get the flat iron to turn on.

"Here," Nicolette said, hitting a few buttons on the digital display and turning it on with ease.

"You're so good at that," I said.

"I use it almost every day," she said, moving her makeup to the side.

Slight plumes of steam came off of the flat iron as I tried to work quickly and efficiently as to not burn any of my hair off. I must've done a good job, because not a single piece came off, unlike in some videos I'd seen online.

"What are you going to wear?" Nicolette asked.

"Probably something a little more casual. I don't want to show up in the same thing again," I said as I applied my mascara.

"I have something fairly new you could borrow. I think it's hot," she said before leaving the bathroom.

I knew that Nicolette giving me clothes was never a great thing, even though the sentiment behind it was always pure and nice. Nicolette, especially with her going-out attire, didn't exactly dress conservatively. I knew I could expect something that would let my ass break free if I bent over even the slightest bit. That might work well for her, but I didn't like my goods being shown about, and I knew that Blake wouldn't appreciate it, either.

"Here," she said as she held up a blue dress.

"Wow, that's actually not half-bad," I said as I looked at it with amazement.

It would show some cleavage, but it actually went down to my knees, and I knew that I'd look pretty good for Blake. I guess she did come through for me this time.

"Just don't mess it up. I'll kill you if you do. I just got it," she said.

"I'll treat it as if it were my own. Besides, I'm sure Blake would get you a new one if it got messed up," I said.

"Hm, on that thought, mess it up. I bet I could get a nicer one," she said with a joking tone, even though we both knew she wasn't totally joking.

After taking off my robe, I slipped into the dress before walking out to a smiling Nicolette, who put her thumbs up. I did a little spin, letting her see it from all angles as I asked her how I looked in it.

"You look great, Penny, you really do. You'll knock him dead, and I'll be shocked if he doesn't fuck you after seeing you in that dress," she said.

"Is that the only thing ever on your mind?" I asked.

"Hey! I haven't gotten any in a while, and I'm living vicariously through you, so deal with it," she replied.

I rolled my eyes and grabbed my purse before taking it over to the front door and slipping on my shoes. Everything matched perfectly, and that wasn't even planned considering I got this dress last-minute from Nicolette. I liked when things came together like that.

"Is he picking you up?" Nicolette asked.

"No, I'm going to meet him there. I have to get going in a minute, though. I don't want to be late. Every minute I'm late is a minute I don't get to spend with him," I said.

"You're so in love," she said, opening the fridge and pulling out some juice.

"No," I said, brushing it off.

"Yes, you are! Look at you! You're so into this guy it's not even funny. I bet he feels the same way about you, too," she said.

I wanted to say that the entire idea was absurd, but was it? We'd been seeing each other for a while, and even though we'd had our ups and downs, things had gone fairly well, I'd say. We did spend a lot of time together, and we were past the whole awkward phase. Still, though, there was one major flaw to the idea.

"We're not even technically together," I said.

"Yeah, but you will be soon," she replied.

"You don't know that," I said as I fiddled with my purse in my hands.

"I'd bet money on it," she replied.

Nicolette was usually right about this kind of thing, but you have to lose sometime, and I was wondering if she was wrong this time. I knew Blake liked me, a lot even, but there was no way he *loved* me. How did I feel about him, though? I didn't know. I wasn't sure I really knew what love was or what it felt like. I knew that I liked him, a lot, but the word love was a huge step and commitment that I just wasn't sure I was ready to give.

"We'll see," I said before putting my hand on the doorknob.

"Be good tonight, even though I know you'll be naughty," she said as I walked out of the apartment.

Nicolette locked the door behind me and I walked down the slippery stairs and outside where Gustav was patiently waiting for me.

"Good evening, Ms. Wells," he said, opening the door.

"I told you before to call me Penny. I mean it," I said in a friendly tone.

"As you wish, Penny," he replied.

The heater was running and I felt the cool tingle against my legs quickly dissipate once he closed the door. I rubbed my hands together, more out of nervousness than anything, as Gustav got inside the car and strapped himself in.

"Where are we going tonight?" I asked.

"I believe Mr. Hunter wants it to be a surprise," he said, looking back at me in the rearview mirror before pulling off the curb.

As we drove through the streets of San Francisco I looked all around to see if I recognized where we were. Was Blake going to take me somewhere new? Was I going to see him standing outside a place we'd already been to before? Maybe he'd take me to our fun little place where it all began. The anticipation was intense, but I sort of enjoyed being kept on edge.

After about twenty minutes, Gustav pulled over

on the side of the road before turning on his signal and unlocking the car. My door opened and my focus shifted from Gustav's smiling face to the person opening the door. It was Blake.

"Hello, beautiful," he said as he extended his hand.

I grabbed it and was led out of the car, where I stood on a familiar sidewalk.

"The bug place?" I asked with a smile.

"The bug place," he replied.

"I thought you hated coming here," I said.

"I wanted to take you back to where it all began," he said.

"Where what began?" I asked, confused.

"Where I knew I'd found the one," he replied, closing the car door behind me.

A rush of emotions flooded through my body as I felt my skin tingling and my face flush. Smiling, I held his hand and followed him inside the restaurant, where a man in a suit was waiting for us.

"Good evening, and welcome to you both. I am Gene St. Claude, and I am the general manager. We're very honored and excited to have you both here tonight, and we're very happy that you've chosen to dine with us again. If you'd please follow me, I'll be escorting you to your table," Gene said.

"You're really all full of surprises, aren't you?" I whispered as we walked behind Gene.

"The biggest one is still to come," he said, and I felt goose-bumps form over my body.

"Here we are. A private table for two," Gene said as he set the menus down on our table.

"Thank you very much, Gene," Blake said.

"It is my pleasure, Mr. Hunter. Your waitress, Nicole, will be with you shortly. Once again, thank you for dining with us again. Enjoy."

We were at the same table as last time, or at least I thought it was the same table. As usual, we were in a secluded spot, but I could hear children in the next room gasping as they likely found out for the first time that their meal was really chock-full of creepy crawlers that were trying to poke out wherever they could. I was almost nervous myself to have to go through it again, but I was more excited at the fact that Blake left his comfort zone again to come to a place like this. And what was that about the biggest surprise still yet to come?

"Good evening, how are you two doing tonight?" a woman, who I guessed to be Nicole, asked.

"Wonderful, and yourself?" Blake replied.

"I'm doing well, thank you. Can I start you off with some drinks? Are we celebrating anything tonight?" Nicole asked.

"Yes to drinks, and hopefully to the celebrating," Blake said.

"Congratulations early. What can I get you to drink?" Nicole asked.

"I'll have the tropical lemonade, but can you spike it? Maybe some of your finest rum?" Blake asked.

"We certainly can. And for you?" Nicole said.

"I'll have the same. It sounds good," I said.

"Great. I'll get those for you and be right back. If you have any questions after looking over the menu, please let me know!"

Though Blake kept bringing up some surprise and telling Nicole he hoped we'd be celebrating something tonight, he didn't say a word after she left. He looked over the menu like nothing was going on tonight and left me absolutely hanging. He wasn't going to do *it* tonight, was he? He wasn't going to ask me to be his girlfriend. He couldn't. Well, he could, but would he really do it here? I was glad I didn't bet money with Nic.

"What looks good to you?" Blake asked.

"I'm not sure," I said, before I started to actually look at the menu.

"I'm liking the bison meatloaf with the crushed cricket and breadcrumb crust. Even comes with mashed potatoes, green beans, and a side of pan-fried mealworms. Yum," he said, with obvious sarcasm at the end.

"I could go for the baja chicken tacos with the ant salsa," I said as I looked at the somewhat appetizing picture inside.

"A woman who takes risks—I like it," he said.

"Okay, here you guys go. I have your drinks for you," Nicole said, setting them down in front of us.

The swirl of colors ran throughout the glass as a twist of my straw made them meld together, ruining the picture-perfect look.

"Have you two decided on something?" Nicole asked.

"I'm ready," I said.

"Ladies first," Blake said, extending his hand.

"I'll have the baja chicken tacos," I said as I

pointed to it on the menu.

"Excellent choice. And for you?" she asked.

"I'll have the bison meatloaf meal," Blake said.

"One of my personal favorites. You'll love it. I'll have someone bring out some complimentary house bread and get the orders in for you right away," Nicole said before walking away.

"So, what is tonight about?" I asked confidently.

"What do you mean?" Blake asked.

"Well, you told people about a surprise or celebration tonight. Did something happen? Did the merger finalize?" I asked.

"No, not yet, unfortunately. I had something else in mind to celebrate tonight," he said.

"Oh? What's that, exactly? Should I be scared?" I asked with a smile.

"Maybe, maybe not. I guess you'll just have to wait and find out," he said, smirking.

"No, tell me!" I said, pouting like one of the kids in the restaurant.

"It'll spoil everything if I tell. You'll just have to wait until dessert," he said, before catching himself.

"Oh, so that's the time, huh? So maybe I should just shovel my food down my throat so I can get to dessert, then," I said.

"I have to get done with my meal too, you know," he said.

"Yeah, yeah, whatever you say," I replied, tapping my fingers on the table.

"So, what did you do today?" he asked before taking a sip of his lemonade.

"Not too much. I was just coding before I got

ready for the date," I replied.

"Coding? What are you working on?" he asked.

"Just some dumb game I've been working on for a few years. It's just a fun thing to do to pass the time and keep my skills fresh," I said.

"I'd love to see and play it sometime if you'd let me," he said.

"Eh," I replied, shifting in my seat.

"If you don't want to, you don't have to, but I'd love to see it if you'd let me," he said.

"How come you want to see it?" I asked.

"Because it's something you're working on and I'm interested in your work. I want to be supportive and help you achieve your goals and dreams," he said.

"It's not like I plan on ever doing anything with it," I said.

"How come?" he asked.

"Because it's just a dumb little game. Nobody would even care about it, anyway," I said.

"That's not true. I bet it's a fun, addictive game and tons of people would like it. I won't press the issue any more, but if you ever want to publish it, I'll help you. I don't mind at all," he said.

"Thank you. It means a lot to me," I said as a man came up beside me and dropped off our bread assortment and some plates.

The breads, which were rustic looking, came with whipped butter, regular butter, and oil with pepper on the side. I broke off a piece of the bread, dipped it in a tiny bit of oil, and took a bite before it melted against my taste buds and made me want to close my eyes.

"This is really good," I said with my mouth still half full.

"I wonder what's in it. It is pretty tasty," Blake said.

Before replying, I ripped off another piece and picked up a knife before slathering some of the whipped butter on top. I couldn't get it to my mouth fast enough before I felt the coolness of the butter against my tongue. I think I waited too long between meals before coming here. I definitely should've eaten lunch because now I just looked like a hungry dog.

While waiting for our meals to arrive, Blake and I talked about everything from school and work to new movies that were coming out that we wanted to see. I said I wanted to see the new one with Kurt Simmons coming out next week, and he said he'd call the director to see if he could get a home copy sent to him. I didn't know that was a thing before he told me, but apparently with enough money and notoriety anything is possible.

After checking on us once and refilling Blake's glass, Nicole soon came out with our food. The aroma alone was enough to make me salivate. Blake's meatloaf looked delicious, especially the gravy-soaked mashed potatoes, and my tacos were jam-packed with cabbage slaw, cilantro, chicken, the ant salsa, avocado, and a creamy ranch sauce that was drizzled in a zigzag formation on top of each taco.

"Is there anything else I can get you?" Nicole asked as she looked back and forth at us.

"Need anything?" Blake asked, looking at me.

"Nope, I think I'm good," I said.

"Same here," Blake replied.

"If you need anything, just let me know!" Nicole said before walking away.

I could feel the warmth of the freshly cooked chicken as it pierced through the flour tortilla against my fingers. Sauce and juices oozed out of the back as I pinched it together and tried to stop the contents from slipping out. I succeeded, though just barely, as I took my first bite and got a little ranch sauce on my upper lip.

"How is it?" Blake asked as he cut his meatloaf a little smaller.

"Oh my god, it's amazing," I said, licking the sauce off of my lip.

Biting into his, Blake kept eye contact with me before closing his eyes and exhaling deeply through his nose. I didn't even have to reciprocate the question.

"I can't even taste the crickets," he said as he crumbled some with his fork.

"Yeah, the ants aren't detectable in my salsa. They do such a good job of blending the flavors and making sure you don't taste them at all," I said.

"So, are you glad I brought you here?" Blake asked.

"For the food, yes, I am. For the surprise, I'm not quite sure. I still don't know what you have planned," I said.

"I'm *fairly* certain that you'll like what I have in store. Would I ever steer you wrong?" he asked.

"No, I guess not," I said, even though I knew he had in the past.

The meal was quiet, as no other tables were too close to us. One older couple was about ten or fifteen feet away, but other than that it was like Blake and I were in our own little rainforest with the décor they had all around us. I always loved themed restaurants so much, especially when they were a little off the wall and goofy.

We ate our meal at a fairly leisurely rate. I had Nicole bring me a water instead of having another lemonade, which was making me a little buzzed. Blake was almost done with his second, and I made him get some water instead of a third one even though he said he was barely even buzzed. It's better to be safe than sorry.

Just after we finished our meals and pushed our plates forward, Nicole came and picked them up, asking if we'd like dessert. She was looking at Blake the entire time. He looked at her, at me, and then back at her.

"Yes, I think we would like some," he said before she left with the plates.

"What was that about?" I asked.

"Oh, nothing. I just like to be friendly," he said.

"Yeah, I bet," I replied.

Nicole soon came out with a molten brownie cake that had vanilla ice cream, whipped cream, and hot fudge oozing out of the sides. Two cherries were on top, one for each of us, and there were two spoons, one stuck in either side. She set it down, smiling, and walked away. I was left with even more questions that I knew I wouldn't get answers to.

"Dig in," he said as he picked up a spoon.

I did the same, taking off a chunk of the brownie cake and snagging some whipped cream and ice cream covered in hot fudge. I barely had any room in my stomach from those tacos and bread, but I couldn't help myself around chocolate—especially molten chocolate. It was like a drug that I wanted to be addicted to.

"So, I've been thinking a lot lately," he said.

Oh god, here it was, and while I had whipped cream all over my face. I quickly wiped it away, not wanting the moment to be ruined as I sat there nervously, listening intently.

"You and I have been through a lot during our time together. We've had ups and very bad downs, but I think we both agree that we stuck it out and it was the best decision. I know I haven't always been the easiest to be with, and you could've left me so many times, but you didn't. You worked it out with me, and we're having the best time of our lives right now," he said.

"I agree. I really enjoy what we have together," I said, my hands placed neatly in my lap.

"But what I want, what I want with you, is so much more than that. Right now I'm nothing but some guy you're dating. You're not mine, and I'm not yours. We're not each other's in any true sense of the word, at least not officially. I want to change that," he said.

"Yeah?" I asked, feeling my cheeks warming up.

"I guess what I'm asking is if you'll be my girlfriend. To take this to the next level and commit one-hundred-percent to one another and be totally exclusive. Not that we weren't before, but you know, officially," he said.

I sat there looking him in the eyes after he asked me what I'd waited so long to hear. I didn't have any burning secrets to tell him this time that would ruin us, and he didn't have anything that would hurt me. We were in the best possible spot we'd ever been in, and as I looked him in the eyes, I knew I wanted it more than anything. I wanted *him* more than anything.

"Yes," I said, smiling.

"Yes?" he asked, a smile growing on his face.

"Absolutely yes," I said.

Leaning over the table, he kissed me slowly, and I felt a flood of emotions barrel over, through, and across my body. It finally happened. We were finally together.

CHAPTER TWELVE

Blake

My life had seemingly come full circle in what felt like an instant. Penny and I had been together for a while now, going through our ups and downs, trying to make sense of it all, and now all that trial and error seemed to have paid off.

Sure, we should've and could've been here a long time ago, but I think it was better to have it late than never, and believe me, we were looking at never having it. First I lied to her, then she lied to me, and then we finally moved past it all and made peace with ourselves and with each other.

As I looked across the table and matched eyes with her, I couldn't help but feel a sense of relief and joy as the woman looking back at me, the one I'd just kissed, was finally mine. I'd be able to introduce her as my girlfriend, she'd introduce me to her friends and family as her boyfriend, and hopefully this would be just the first step to a longer amount of time together, which as of now I hoped would never end.

After about ten minutes of smiling and talking, Nicole brought the check and we paid before walking out of the restaurant hand in hand. The general manager, who was still there, thanked us for coming, and as we walked out, Gustav was waiting just like I'd planned.

"I thought you drove here," she said.

"Nope, I sent him to get you after he dropped me off here. I wanted to make sure we could celebrate tonight without worrying about driving," I said.

"The celebration is just about to get started," she said, getting into the car.

I walked around to the other side and got in before putting on my seatbelt and wrapping my arm around Penny. She cozied up to me, her body against mine, as her right hand reached up and held onto my hand that was hanging over her shoulder. I caught her looking at me briefly, as I could sense her loving gaze before I turned to her, locked eyes, and kissed her softly. She smiled as I did so, our lips still pushed together, causing me to do the same before I pulled back and looked at her again. She was beautiful.

Gustav pulled into my garage and I got out of my side before walking around the car and opening the door for her. She grabbed my hand upon exiting, and I waved goodbye to Gustav before he pulled out of the lot and back into the street.

The elevator doors opened instantly and it

seemed as though we couldn't keep our hands off of one another as we entered it. Her arms were wrapped around me, her head was pushed up against my chest, and as I kissed her forehead, I finally felt as if the curse was broken. I was no longer the playboy billionaire who could have any girl he wanted. I was the more mature billionaire who had exactly the girl he wanted.

"Have any champagne?" she asked as we walked into my apartment.

"Of course. Wanting to celebrate?" I asked.

"I believe this is an appropriate night to celebrate," she said.

Opening my cooler, I pulled out a bottle of champagne and uncorked it. Standing with two glasses, Penny tilted them as I slowly poured in the fizzing champagne. The foam soon subsided and I set down the opened bottle on the countertop before taking my glass from her and watching the bubbles fly.

"To us," I said as I raised my flute.

"To us," she replied, doing the same.

We gently clinked our glasses together and brought them up to our lips, and I felt the fizzing bubbles pop against my upper lip and nose before I took a sip and reveled in the taste.

Penny made a sour face before swallowing hers and coughing a little.

"Too much for you?" I asked, smiling.

"Nope, just right," she said, setting her flute on the counter.

"Come here," I said, setting my flute down,

before pulling her close and kissing her gently.

She didn't waste any time at all. As her tongue found its way into my mouth I could still taste the bubbles that lay dormant on her tongue. I put my hand against her jaw and pushed back her hair as her hands, looking for something to grab onto, gripped my biceps and squeezed them gently. I could feel the excitement and ecstasy flowing through my veins, as I seemed to know what was going to come next tonight.

"Want to take this upstairs?" I asked.

"Yes, but not just anywhere," she said.

"The bedroom?" I asked.

"Not the bedroom, but a *special* room up there we haven't used in a while," she said.

I hadn't used that room since that night with her, almost forgetting it was up there, but I couldn't forget the fun and toys that were inside.

"Let's go," I replied.

CHAPTER THIRTEEN

Penelope

Even though I had the dampening effects of liquor in my system, I still felt a little nervous as Blake led me to his room. I'd only barely ever been in there even though I'd craved it more times than I can count. What was I nervous about, though? I couldn't quite figure that out. I knew this time in his room was going to be a lot different than the first time in there, and that it might be better, if that was even possible.

We walked up the stairs and towards the room before he opened the door and turned on the dimmed lights. The rows of books surrounded me again and I felt butterflies in my stomach as he walked over to the *special* book, the one that opened the staircase to his small secret floor.

He looked at me as he pulled the book out and

unlocked the door, and it hinged open to reveal a small staircase. I couldn't believe this was happening again.

"After you," he said, with his hand out.

Confidently, I walked past him and up the stairs into his room. The lights turned on, although dim like last time, and I saw the rows of toys on the walls. The dressers and bed were completely made and not unkempt the slightest bit. A flood of emotions, good ones, came over me as I smelled the woodsy scent I discovered the first time I was here. I was almost conditioned to get wet when it hit my nose.

"Nervous?" he asked as I turned around to see him standing right behind me.

"Nervous? Why would I be nervous?" I asked, feeling my hands get a little clammy.

"For what I'm about to do to you," he replied, grabbing me at the waist and pulling me in.

I tasted his lips as he pressed them against mine. He didn't hold back. His hands, firm and strong, gripped my ass before slapping it and sending a shockwave up my spine. He didn't apologize; he didn't need to. Then I knew I was about to be with the old Blake, the no-holds-barred sexual Blake, and I *loved* it.

"Is that all you've got?" I asked, taunting him.

He slapped my ass harder. A red handprint and broken blood vessels would be soon to follow, though I didn't care about any of it. I only wanted him in this moment, and I wanted him bad.

We both gasped for air between kissing like we were drowning inside each other. His hands ran across my body without regard as I pushed mine against his hard, muscular body and wished it were on top of me already.

Blake tugged at my dress, pulling it upwards to expose my bare ass, my red lace thong gripping it tightly, and I felt his hard dick growing against me.

"I want it," I whispered.

"Then come get it," he said in a strong voice.

I grasped his belt buckle and made quick work of it before unzipping his pants and letting them fall to the floor. He kicked them off, some thin boxer briefs now the only thing guarding him from me. I grabbed his waistband and pulled it down slowly as I got down on my knees. He grabbed a pillow, tossing it down for me to kneel on, as I got onto my knees and was quickly met by his spring-loaded cock as it shot out of its confinement.

"Fuck," I said. It looked bigger than I remembered.

I put it up to my forearm, inspecting its length, as I wondered how in the hell this thing even fit inside me. Looking up at him and seeing his obvious enjoyment at my worship of his cock, I gripped his shaft firmly and licked the very tip of his head. His eyes softened before I swirled my tongue all around his head and I saw little bits of my spit glistening all around.

He ran his fingers through my hair and pulled it back as little strands kept getting stuck in my mouth. I didn't break eye contact with him, even when he started to gently thrust his hips and put his loaded dick further and further down my throat. In fact, I kind of liked it.

"Get up," he soon said, as he grabbed my hands and pulled me upwards.

He pulled my dress over my body with ease before pulling down my panties as I unclasped my bra. The tip of his dick pushed against me as he leaned forward and sucked on my nipples slowly, pulling them into his mouth. I bit my lower lip and tried to hold back my moans.

"Give me that pussy," he said as he lay back on the bed.

I got into sixty-nine, my pussy pushed up near his face, as I held myself up with my hands and sucked his dick straight up and down. I soon felt his warm bumpy tongue running circles around my growing clit as I closed my eyes and stopped sucking with half of him inside me. Fuck, it felt good, and it made me want to jump on top of his cock without so much as a warning.

I felt him spread my ass apart with his hands as his tongue wandered all along my pussy, making sure not to discriminate against any part of it. It was like he was making love to my most sensitive areas, and I wasn't about to stop it.

With my arms getting tired of holding myself up, I got down on my forearms as I felt him push his open lips onto my clit and suck with all his might. My right eye twitched, a few sputters of moans escaped my throat, and I swear I had a stroke before he finally broke his grip and let me breathe again.

"Fuck," I whispered

After he licked me until my knees almost gave

way, I got off of Blake and lay back on the bed as he got up and walked over to a dresser, making me anxious. What was he going to pull out this time? What was I going to get?

He closed the dresser drawer, the absence of almost all light in the room hiding what he had in his hands. He got a little bit closer and revealed them to me. Handcuffs, a blindfold, and a whip with black leather tassels were all set on top of the bed.

He placed the blindfold over my eyes, cutting off my vision, and handcuffed my arms to the bed posts. I could feel my pussy beginning to cream before he even got a hold of me. I soon felt his presence as I heard him roll a condom down his hard dick. His hands gripped the bottoms of my thighs, pushing them upwards, and his latex-wrapped dick pressed against my pussy, a few drops of his spit splashing against it to provide some much-needed lube.

Biting my lower lip, I waited, my fists clenched, as I tried to anticipate when he was going to fuck me already. He instead teased me, rubbing his shaft up and down my fleshy lips, and I wanted to tell him to do it.

Right before I was going to beg him to fuck me, I felt his large cock start to stretch me out as he slowly entered my tightened pussy and made me feel like a woman.

"Jesus," I moaned, as if I were feeling him again for the first time.

"You're so fucking tight," he said as he began to slowly thrust himself further inside me.

Every thrust made me moan like I never had

before. I didn't know if it was the mood, the room, or the fact that I was so into him, but something he was doing made this feel the most amazing of all the sex we'd had, and trust me, we'd fucked a lot.

Pushing my legs against his body, he got up on his feet, still bent over, and began to push his entire cock into me. I grasped for the sheets but couldn't hold onto them. I felt his balls slap against my asshole as my nipples hardened as much as they could and my juices began to drip out of my pussy onto the sheets below.

With my thighs against his shoulders, he reached forward, grabbing my tits, and squeezed my nipples gently. I moaned, begging for more, as the feeling of his entire dick deep inside me made me feel like nothing ever had before.

"I'm not sure how much longer I can last," Blake said. I felt him panting for air.

"Give it to me," I moaned, each thrust from him making my tits bounce up and down.

His sweaty body pushed against mine and I let out a long-winded moan when I felt the warmth of his body. Our moment together felt as primal as two people could get, and I knew that we were connected in more ways than one right now. We weren't two souls in this moment, but one.

As Blake began to slow down, his thrusts becoming less and less frequent, I knew what was coming next. There was only one thing left to come, and that was *him*.

He moaned softly as he grabbed my breasts and squeezed them like he meant business. I smiled, feeling his cock bulging inside me. The rush of ecstasy seemed to make him grow even thicker, if that was possible.

He slowed down, his hands leaving me, before he pulled out completely and pulled off the condom, and I felt him moving the bed as he started to jerk himself off. It didn't take long, not even ten seconds, before he held his breath, a moan escaping him, and his hot, sticky load shot all over my stomach. A few of the streams made it all the way up to my sweat-covered tits.

"Yes," I said, as each pump turned me on even more than the last.

His streams soon slowed down and finally ended. He let go of his held breath and squeezed his shaft before slapping his head down on me.

"Fuck," he said, gasping for air.

"Was I a good girl for you?" I asked.

"You're always the best," he replied before pulling my blindfold off.

With my eyes squinted, I soon adjusted to the light in the room and looked down as I saw the giant mess he made all over me. Some of it dripped down my sides before he got up to get a towel and cleaned me up. I waited for him to undo the handcuffs, but he didn't. Instead he went over to his dresser after tossing away the cum-soaked towel and pulled something out.

"What's that?" I asked, intrigued.

"You're never going to leave here without finishing," he said as he pulled something out of a black velvet bag.

He pulled out a dildo, one that spun and had bumps, ridges, and a clit stimulator all on the front. I was a bit nervous, never having used anything like *this* before, but at the same time, I was excited that I had a man who didn't only think of himself.

He turned it on, the vibrations easily heard, before he pushed it up against me and made me arch my back instantly.

"Fuck!" I screamed, sputtering out bursts of air.

"Yeah, come for me, baby," he said as he pushed the dildo end of it inside me.

It wasn't nearly as big or thick as him, but the bumps and ridges sure helped as they spun inside me and made me squirm. I could barely contain myself, not even for a few minutes, before the pulsating V that was on the tip of the device tickled my already swollen clit and sent shockwaves throughout my body.

It was coming; *I* was coming. As I gripped the chains of the handcuffs and arched my back like I was being exorcised, I felt my pussy clench up around his dildo as I let out a moaning scream that was sure to penetrate the walls and wake the neighbors.

"Fuck," I heard him say.

After seven seconds I gasped for air, my arms getting tired, before another one came without warning and made my pussy tense up to the point that I didn't know if he'd be able to keep it inside me. He soon pulled it out, the vibrations leaving my clit, and I fell back down to the bed and felt the cold sweat-stained sheets under me.

Blake unlocked the handcuffs and tossed them

aside. I rubbed my wrists and rested as my heart rate finally started to come down. With a washcloth in hand, Blake patted my forehead and face dry before leaning in and kissing me softly.

"How was that?" he asked.

"Was it as good for you as it was for me?" I asked.

"Oh, I don't think so," he said, laughing. "I don't think anybody on this planet has ever felt *that* good."

Smiling, I motioned for him to come down and I kissed him once again as my hands ran through the back of his soaked hair.

Tonight had easily been the best night of my life.

I lay awake in Blake's arms later that night as he peacefully slept—even snoring a little at one point, though that quickly stopped.

Small rays of moonlight shone through his curtains and onto our naked bodies as we embraced underneath the covers and kept one another warm. I liked sleeping with him like this, not because we were naked, but because I thought it brought us closer together.

With my arms wrapped tightly around his torso, I rested my head against his chest and listened to his heartbeat, one thump at a time, as I closed my eyes. He really wore me out earlier, and I knew that I needed to get some rest if I was going to be able to wake up in the morning. Part of me just wanted to stay awake and listen to his heartbeat, even though it was getting harder and harder to keep my eyes open.

After about five minutes, I couldn't go on any longer, and with my head still flush against his chest, I finally fell back asleep in his arms.

"Good morning, you," I heard as I opened my groggy eyes.

I looked up and saw Blake on his phone, my arms still wrapped around him, though he was sitting up at an angle.

"Good morning," I said before letting go of him and stretching every muscle I could.

I took a deep breath in, then let it out. I could feel the bags under my eyes, as I hadn't gotten enough sleep. I didn't even know what time it was, but judging that the sun didn't rise until later in the morning this time of year, it must have been late enough. Maybe I'd just have one of those somewhat tired days.

"I was wondering when you'd get up. How'd you sleep?" he asked.

"I slept well, though I'm still a bit tired and a little hungry," I said.

"Want breakfast?" he asked.

"If you're making it," I replied with a smile.

"Of course. I'll go start and you come down when you're ready," he said before getting out of bed and putting some pajama pants on.

I watched him walk out of the room as I tried to wake myself up and not let myself fall back asleep. I sometimes had a tendency of doing that if I kept lying down, and I knew that it was time to get up and conquer the day.

Sitting up in bed, I grabbed my phone from the nightstand and checked my messages and e-mail. Nicolette texted me once, but it was just a funny picture of some guy on a local commercial we'd laughed about once. I smiled and texted her back before locking my phone and swinging my legs out of the bed.

I walked into his closet and picked out some of my clothes before slipping them on and sliding my feet into some slippers he'd bought for me the other day. They were soft and fuzzy, microfiber, I thought, and they felt like a cloud. I shuffled my feet as I walked out of the room and downstairs, where I heard the sizzling sound of bacon in a skillet before I turned and saw him frying up a feast.

"All of that for us?" I asked.

"You said you were hungry," he said as he flipped a pancake.

"Hungry—not starving," I whispered under my breath.

I poured some orange juice into a large jar he had for drinks and brought it over to the table before doing some cooking of my own and making us toast. It was burnt a little on the edges, which was a bit embarrassing considering Blake was cooking all this for us and he'd made it all perfectly. I'm a failure in the kitchen. My grandmother would be embarrassed.

"Sit down, I'll bring it to the table," he said.

I walked over and sat down as he made us two plates, even though there was more than enough food for two more people.

"Here you go," he said as he set it down in front of me.

The plate was filled with scrambled eggs, extra-crispy bacon, buttermilk pancakes, the toast I made, and some fresh fruit. I felt full before I even took my first bite just from looking at it all.

"Thank you. It looks delicious," I said as I put my napkin in my lap and picked up my silverware.

I slathered some butter on my pancakes and slid it around before cutting them up and dripping some pure maple syrup on top. The syrup dripped onto some of my bacon as well, making a delicious treat that I just had to try first.

Crunchy and a little sticky, the bacon broke apart in my mouth before my saliva melded with it and took me to a place of bliss. Bacon had become so popular in the past few years, and this was exactly why. It was amazing, and I would've been content with a plate of just bacon for breakfast.

"So, I was thinking we could go out and do something fun today," Blake said.

"Oh yeah?" I asked.

"I need to do some shopping for some new clothes, and I was hoping you'd come help me pick some out," he said, putting some food in his mouth.

"You want me to help? I'm not exactly fashion-forward, you know. I might mess it up," I said.

"Nonsense. I think you have a good eye for fashion, and besides, I want to look good for you and that's best achieved with you picking out some of my outfits," he said.

"That's sweet of you to say. I'll definitely try my best, though I'm not promising you're going to come out looking amazing. I'm still new at this," I said.

Blake and I took a leisurely amount of time to eat our breakfast as he read the business section of the paper and I read the humor section. That definitely showed the contrast between us, though I don't think that matters. Sometimes it's a good thing to be with somebody who's the exact opposite of you. It brings you out of your comfort zone and introduces you to new things and experiences that you likely wouldn't have experienced otherwise.

Later that day, after taking a shower together and goofing around while getting ready, Blake and I got into his sports car and pulled out of the garage before heading to one of his favorite stores.

A sales associate greeted us as we walked into the all-white sterile store that felt more like a hospital with clothes on the walls than anything else. There was a variety of clothing, from suits to casual wear, as well as all the accessories the budding young billionaire could ever need. I looked at some of the clothes, seeing that a black t-shirt was priced at a hundred dollars, and almost choked on my spit before Blake came over and rubbed the middle of my back and helped me come back. Money really was no object for him.

"I think we'll take it from here, Joshua. If I need

something, I'll be sure to ask," Blake said to the sales associate.

"Not a problem, sir. Let me know if you need anything at all," Joshua said before walking away.

"See anything you like?" Blake asked.

"There's a lot of nice stuff, but I think I have to look around a little bit more," I said.

I slowly walked along the wall and ran my fingers along the bevy of crisp button-up shirts that hung from a stainless steel rod. They were in all different colors and patterns, and I found a light blue linen one that I thought would look good on him.

"I like this," I said as I held it up.

"Yeah, it would be a nice casual one. We can get it," he said.

"Don't you want to try it on to make sure it fits and you like it?" I asked.

"I usually don't bother," he said, continuing to browse undershirts that were laid out on a table.

As the two of us shopped, I found a few other shirts and a pair of flat shorts that would be good for late spring and summer. He picked out some V-neck shirts, the rich ones that I choked upon seeing, and a few ties that he said would switch up his look for work. I'd noticed that he'd had much more variety in his wardrobe since we got together, but I wasn't sure if that was because of me or not. Maybe it was just a coincidence.

"How do you like these?" he asked, holding up a dark gray pair of sneakers.

"They look good. I think they'd match your new shirts and shorts well," I said.

"Do you have these in a twelve?" Blake asked Joshua.

"Yes, sir. Let me go get them for you," he said, going into the back.

Two other workers took all the clothes we picked up and took them to the counter as Joshua came back out with the shoes.

"Would you like to try them on?" he asked.

"No, that won't be necessary. I trust they'll fit. Did you like anything else?" Blake asked, looking at me.

"No, I think that was it," I replied.

"I believe that will be it for us," Blake said.

Nodding, Joshua began to ring everything up as the other workers started to fold and wrap everything. Blake took out his wallet, waiting for the total, as I just stood there and watched the total climb.

"Okay, that will be $3,456.78," Joshua said.

My jaw tried to drop but the pure shock of the total kept it tightly hinged to my skull. How in the hell did this shit cost that much? We could've gone anywhere else and gotten the same stuff for two hundred dollars, *maybe* three hundred max.

Blake handed his black card to Joshua, who quickly swiped it and returned it to him. Blake signed the receipt, handed it to him, and put his wallet away.

"The items will be delivered later today to your residence. Thank you once again, Mr. Hunter. It's always a pleasure," Joshua said.

"Likewise, and have a good day," Blake said before grabbing my hand and walking out of the store.

"What now?" I asked as we walked outside.

"How about a little something for you?" he asked.

"I suppose I could do that," I said, thinking of how I needed a new dress. "No super fancy places, though. A department store is just fine."

"As you wish. Any ideas?" he asked.

"Yeah, one," I said, thinking of the store where I was supposed to have had a job not too long ago.

People looked at Blake and me as we walked into the store and heard the faint sound of elevator music playing in the background. I could see some of them whispering, not because we were together, but because he was here in this store. I didn't know he was as well known by the public as he apparently was, but I tried not to let it bother me. I guess this was a small price I'd have to sometimes pay for dating somebody of his stature.

"I want to get a new dress for when we go out. I'm sick of wearing the same one all the time," I said.

"Well, it looks like the women's section is upstairs," he said as we looked at a store map.

Taking the escalator up, I was reminded of when I came here for that interview. I wondered if I'd see anyone from that day, maybe one of the other applicants spraying perfume or performing another function, but I didn't, at least not that I knew of.

There was a separate section for dresses of all types, from formal to casual, and even prom dresses that were out early with sale prices. They all hung from a myriad of wall poles and carousels spread all around with large red signs that read "sale" or "discount". I knew Blake didn't care about spending the money at a nicer place if I wanted to go there, but I was still a little weird about him buying me things anyway. I was getting better, a lot better, but I was so used to being fully independent and poor that getting new things was a bit of an adjustment.

"I like this one," I said as I picked up a pale pink dress that was tighter in the bust and flowing in the bottom.

It didn't show any cleavage, and it even had some texture in the top. I knew it'd be nice to wear to a dinner or even to meet more of his friends or family.

"It's nice, I like it," he said.

"Would you still think I was cute if I wore this?" I asked.

"I think you'd look *beautiful* if you were in that," he replied.

Smiling, I handed it to him and had him hold onto it as I kept looking at some of the sale and clearance rack items. The dresses looked like a rainbow as I ran through them and picked out a few more that could be used for a variety of occasions. There were sexy ones, conservative ones, and some that were kind of in the middle. Blake liked them all, and since they were marked down I didn't feel too bad having him get them.

After about half an hour in the store, and noticing he looked bored, I decided to call it a day and we walked downstairs to pay. The girl at the counter, who looked about my age, scanned all the tags and took off the security tags. When the price came up on the screen I could see a look of confusion on Blake's face.

"That will be $74.32," the woman said.

"That's it?" Blake asked as he looked at me.

"That's it," I replied, smiling back at him.

He handed her his black card and she swiped it before he got the receipt and looked it over again.

"I can't believe all that was so cheap," he said.

"Hey, that's what you get for buying sale and clearance items," I said.

"But you got five dresses. Surely there must be a mistake somewhere," he said.

"Nope, no mistake. You even scored another twenty percent off for our weekend sale," the cashier said.

"Wow," he replied, grabbing the stuffed bag from the counter.

"Maybe you're going to the wrong place," I said as we walked away.

"Maybe I am," he replied.

Blake and I went to lunch after shopping and talked a lot about anything and everything we could think of. He told me he made our travel plans, and that we'd leave in less than two weeks. As I heard him tell me it was set in stone, I felt a bit of nerves come over me.

What if his family didn't like me? I knew that they didn't have a ton of bearing in his life and he cared more about his own opinion than anyone else's, but I didn't want them to hate me or something. Maybe they wouldn't think I was good enough for him or that our small age difference was too large, or there would be something else that wouldn't spell good news for me. I didn't want to dread seeing them in the future, if Blake and I were even still together. I guess I'd always dreamt about being loved and accepted by a boyfriend or husband's family, and that they'd sort of become the family I wished I had growing up. A happy, cohesive unit who were always there for one another.

"Is your family friendly?" I asked as we sipped our coffee.

"I guess as much as someone can be. They aren't in-your-face happy and friendly, but they definitely aren't mean or anything like that—at least my mom isn't," he said.

"But your dad is mean?" I asked.

"No, not exactly, but he's more of a reserved man, I'd say, and I think that it comes off the wrong way sometimes. He just doesn't like to be the center of attention," he said.

"Kind of like me, I guess," I said.

"Exactly like you, so I'm willing to bet you two will get along just fine," he said.

"What about your friends back home? Will I be meeting any of them?" I asked.

"Possibly, we'll see. I don't have many friends back there, at least ones who I want to see, but there are a few who are good, especially Jeremy," he said.

"Who's he?" I asked.

"A friend who lived down the street from me growing up. We were always good friends, but I wouldn't say best friends or anything. We never shared any deep dark secrets or passions, but we hung out a lot and did stuff together. He stayed in town after graduation and became a mechanic, and he's one of the only people I know from home who hasn't asked me for money or tried to get stuff from me," Blake said.

"Wow, that must be tough, having people ask you for money—especially people you don't see often or talk to," I said.

"It can be, but it's to be expected. It's kind of like when you win the lottery, but I guess not as bad. With that people think you didn't earn it, so they feel you must share it, but with mine I built it from the ground up and they know that, so they aren't as grabby. Maybe it's a little different with my case, though, since I have so much—especially in comparison to a lottery winner."

"Do you stay in contact with any of them outside of being home?" I asked.

"No, not really. None of them have my number, at least none that I know of. We don't have much in common, especially now with the company and my lifestyle, so it's best to just go our separate ways and maybe see each other every once in a while when I'm visiting," he said.

"That's rough. I'm happy you'll get to see them, at least the ones worth seeing. I think it will be interesting to meet people you know who aren't rich or business owners. No offense to Brian and Maggie, I loved them, but they aren't exactly your every-day average people anymore," I said.

"It'll be a stark contrast, that's for sure," he said, taking another sip.

Blake and I spent the remainder of the day walking around the city and going towards the water to see Alcatraz from afar. There were a lot of tourists about, many of them getting on the boat to go to the prison, though we opted not to and instead just took it in as the sun set and cast the sky in a fiery blaze of oranges and yellows.

These simple moments with Blake were some of my favorites. He'd proven to me time and time again that you don't need some fancy dinner or expensive night to have a good time. Sometimes all you need is the person you care about and you can be all right. I think he was figuring that out more and more as time went on, too.

I wasn't going to stay the night tonight, since he had a flight in the morning for a quick business trip up north, but I came back to his place for dinner that he ordered in. He got us Thai food, a big spread, and we ate it in the media room and watched a movie as we snuggled up together and fed some appetizers to each other. I didn't care much about the movie, as it was one he picked that I'd seen before, but I didn't say anything and instead acted like I was super into it. It was more important that he was happy and enjoying himself.

It was almost sad when our night came to a close and it was time for me to go home. I said I'd take a cab, but he insisted on driving me, stating that he was my boyfriend and it was his job to make sure I got home safe. I told him it wasn't necessary, but he wouldn't concede and I finally caved and told him he could take me.

We got into his SUV and I immediately turned on the seat warmers. The leather began to heat up and keep my somewhat frosty butt warm. Traffic wasn't too bad, which was a shame, because I loved just sitting in the car with him, the radio on low, holding his hand as the city lights twinkled all around us. It was just a simple time together that never got old.

After what felt like only a minute, Blake pulled up to my building and I looked up and felt a bit of sadness come over me. I wasn't going to cry, nothing like that, but as I looked back at him and saw him staring at me, I didn't want to leave him. I didn't want him to leave the city for a few days and I just wanted to go back to his place and feel him against me as we cuddled all night long.

"Well, this is it," he said.

"I'm going to miss you. You better not forget about me while you're gone," I said.

"Forget about you? Never. I'll be sure to text you in the morning," he said, holding my hand.

"Good, I'll be waiting for it," I said.

He leaned in, kissed me softly on the lips, and

then backed up and kissed my forehead as I closed my eyes and smiled. I grabbed my things from between my feet, opened the door, and closed it before getting into the building and turning back around.

I saw him waving at me, a frown on his face, as I waved back and he soon pulled off of the curb and drove away. Here's to the next few days without Blake..

CHAPTER FOURTEEN

Blake

There was always work to be done and it seemed I was the one who always had to do it.

I was traveling to Seattle again today to finalize the contracts on the new offices and break the first ground, so to speak. I wasn't required to come, as the contracts could've just been sent to the office, but I insisted on it, as I liked to be a part of everything. After all, I built this company, and I wanted to be present whenever we expanded. It seemed only fitting.

I'd thought about asking Penny to come on this trip with me like she did last time, but she had school soon and I knew she wanted to get a head start on some midterm papers so that she wouldn't have to worry during our trip back home. Besides, I wasn't here long and wouldn't have much time to sight-see. I was going to be missing her badly, but I thought it would only make me appreciate her more when I got back to San Francisco.

As I boarded the jet with two of my business colleagues, I checked my phone one last time and saw that she'd sent me a picture. I opened it and saw her smiling face in bed, the covers up to her chin, the caption inviting me in. I smiled a little, though nobody else saw it, before I replied that I'd love nothing more than to be with her right now. Why couldn't I see that face every morning when I woke up? Maybe someday, if things kept going well. You never know what the future has in store.

I turned off my phone, grabbed my laptop, and turned it on to a podcast that Grace had downloaded for me. The flight attendant brought us breakfast and drinks, though I suppose we were too busy to eat together. Instead they were drowned in paperwork as I sat here and relaxed all the way there. Sometimes it's nice to be the boss.

I caught a glimpse of the mountains as we approached Seattle and I couldn't help but look out the window with my sunglasses on and revel in the majesty that they exuded. It was too bad Penny wasn't here to look as well. I knew she'd like this type of thing.

A large black SUV picked us up on the tarmac and I immediately turned my phone back on and saw a text from Penny saying she hoped I had a good flight and to Skype with her later tonight if I had time. I knew my schedule would be pretty tight even at night, but I could always make time for her. She was worth it.

There was a team of people standing outside the new building as we approached. The landscapers had done a phenomenal job, even though a small half-inch of snow covered the fresh dirt and mulch that had been spread around the facility. They all clapped as we pulled up. They even had a banner with the company name and logo on it, and the front of the building displayed our name and logo too. It was nice seeing it out front and not just in a placard inside the building like at our headquarters.

"Good morning, Mr. Hunter," Kenneth, the man I was here to see, said.

"Good morning, Kenneth. I assume all is well here. Contracts are moving?" I asked.

"Yes, sir. They're inside now waiting for your signature," Kenneth said.

"We'll get to them in a second. First, let's welcome all these people and get them inside for the opening," I said.

I shook all their hands as I read their nametags and surprisingly remembered a few of them from the employee sheet I'd gotten a few days prior. They all seemed happy to meet me, but they might just have been happy to have a job in this market.

As we walked inside, I smelled the fresh paint and wood flooring that was laid throughout the building. When we designed this place, it was important to me that we kept the spirit of Seattle and Washington as a whole and kept the outdoors in as much of the space as we could. This wasn't going to be a sterile working environment, but a different kind of extension of our headquarters back home.

I was shown around the floors, which were laid out just like the other ones. Only a few people had offices of their own, and the rest were in cubicles that offered enough work privacy without completely sectioning people off from their peers. There were beanbag chairs, skateboards, massage chairs, snack bars, and so many more things that I felt were great for keeping happy employees moving.

There were tables with lunch set up, including an ice cream bar and soda fountain manned by old-timey-looking workers to bring the experience fully together.

"Before we begin, how about we go and sign?" Kenneth asked.

"You've been patient enough. Let's go," I said.

Kenneth led my team and me to the largest office in the building and we sat down as he presented the contracts that we'd gone back and forth on many times before. The company's lawyers were there, making sure it was the contract we agreed upon, before cameras were taken out to record this momentous occasion.

"They look good," one of our lawyers said.

Grabbing a pen from a wooden holster, I placed the tip against the paper and took a deep breath in. This moment meant so much to me, and I only wished Penny were here to see it. I would have loved nothing more.

I signed my name on the line and heard the popping of champagne bottles as pictures were taken and I shook hands with everybody. I was handed a glass, as was everyone else, and we all toasted before taking a sip and going out to the rest of the festivities outside.

I'd done it. I'd finally officially expanded the company.

CHAPTER FIFTEEN

Penelope

I spent the morning attempting to make a resume for Maggie, but it was going nowhere. I'd decided to revise the one I used for Blake's company, as it seemed like a good starting place, and I needed to talk more about school in it. I even contemplated just stating I had already graduated and just telling Maggie in the e-mail what I did, since I wouldn't be hired or starting there until after graduation in a couple months anyway.

The cursor on the screen blinked as I failed to type in any of my accomplishments in either school or my professional life. I hadn't held a job in a while, and I had no internships to really talk about. I did well in school, but I wasn't big on clubs or organizations that pertained to my major. I think the only saving grace I had was that Maggie liked me so much. I didn't think this resume would help me all that much with landing a good job somewhere in my field—at least not in this city. If Maggie's place turned me down I *might* need Blake to put in a good word for me. I might not have any other choice.

After wallowing a bunch in my own self-doubt, I reread my resume and made sure it had no glaring mistakes. I put all of my contact information up top and pulled out Maggie's business card nervously before I typed her e-mail address into a new e-mail and typed that it was me and I was giving her my resume. I wasn't expecting a job from her, or even an interview, for that matter, and I'd found it's always better not to expect anything. I'm not owed anything in life, and I think my upbringing definitely taught me that. She may have spoken very highly of me and liked me a lot, but until I had a job offer in my hands to sign, I was still keeping my guard up.

"Are you almost ready?" Nicolette yelled from outside my door as I sent the e-mail.

We had plans to go to some indoor farmer's market/flea market/vintage market thing that she'd seen online. She said they'd have a lot of cool stuff, and she went to one a couple months ago, so I figured I'd tag along since I had nothing else to do and Blake was out of town. I knew I wasn't going to buy anything, but I guessed I could be her pack mule and help her carry the stuff I knew she was going to buy back to her car.

"Ready," I said as I walked out of my room with my purse in my hand.

I locked up and we walked down the street to her car just as the meter was beginning to run low. Her car somewhat smelled like pizza and body spray and I realized I hadn't been in it for a while, so who knows what she'd even been doing in here. Judging by this smell, though, she was spiraling out of control.

The parking was free, though limited, as we had to walk a fair distance to the building the event was in and pay a five-dollar cover charge, which she happily paid for me just for coming with her. Vendors of all sorts were spread about, though it was cramped inside, and many hipster-looking young adults were crowded around the many vintage tents that had cropped up selling the same types of things. Why people purchased old furniture that someone sanded, painted white, and beat with a chain, I'd never know. Maybe I should get into that business. I could probably clean up.

"Oh, come here!" Nicolette said, dragging me over to a stand.

There was an older woman, maybe in her mid-sixties, who sold jars of homemade jams and preserves of all different types. After sampling a few on some wheat crackers, Nicolette bought a mango, peach, and cherry sampler and put them all inside her green canvas bags. The woman was very thankful, as she didn't look to have as many people coming around her tent compared to some others, which sort of made me sad and feel a little bad for her. It seems like sometimes the people with the best and most honest and wholesome things don't always get the attention they deserve.

We shuffled around the tents and Nicolette bought a few more items before she said she was tired and wanted to sit down and eat. There was a food-court-style place here, with local vendors and restaurants cooking up delicious menus, and even though the lines were long, we decided to stay and try them out. We bought a stone-fired margherita pizza and shared it as we sat down on high bar stools and drank diet sodas, which were in those cheap Styrofoam cups that were likely horrible for the environment and never recycled.

"Look at that couple. They match," Nicolette said as she pointed to an older couple.

They were dressed as the United States flag; the man's shirt was blue and had all fifty stars, while the woman had a red and white striped shirt. The two of them together, side by side, completed the flag, and I couldn't help but smile and laugh a bit. I hoped Blake never wanted to wear matching outfits like that.

We had fun people-watching, which was something that we used to do all the time together way back when. We were never mean about it, and we definitely made sure nobody saw us talking about them, but sometimes it was fun to watch the very different kinds of people walking by and point them out to one another.

We'd seen guys with cats on their heads, couples and families in matching outfits, and people with so many tattoos and piercings my head spun. There was always something to see here in San Francisco, and nobody even batted an eye most of the time. Maybe it was because I wasn't born here or hadn't spent enough time here, but some of this stuff still got me every time.

I rubbed my calves a little, trying to get them back in the mood to begin walking around again, before Nicolette said she was ready and we threw away our plates and cups. It wasn't the walking that got me as much as the standing around. I hated that, especially when you're trapped in a crowd of other people doing the same thing. It was claustrophobic and made me wonder what would happen if an emergency of some kind took place. What if there was a fire? We'd all be trapped against each other.

"Oh, this is cute," Nicolette said as we walked up to a booth.

The owner was luckily busy with other customers and couldn't talk to us, and as I looked over Nicolette's shoulder, I rolled my eyes and told her to put it down.

"But it's so cute," she said, holding up a handmade dog collar.

"We don't have a dog, Nicolette. Not sure if you remember," I said.

"Maybe someday we will. Wouldn't it be nice to have a cute collar ready for if that day comes?" she asked.

"No, it wouldn't. I'm vetoing this right now," I said, grabbing her and pulling her away.

Sure, they were cute, and sure, it was fun to look at the different booths, but only when you had a reason to potentially buy something. Buying a collar now because in five years you *might* have a dog was just stupid. It made me wonder how she even had any spare money left at all at the end of the month. I was surprised she didn't have more junk lying around the apartment. Then again, I hadn't been in her room for a while.

I caught a glimpse of another vendor from across the room and walked through the crowd before coming up on a man with a handlebar mustache and slicked and parted hair.

He had many different men's products, like hair stuff, face stuff, shaving stuff, and even cologne. All of it was wrapped in a matte black covering with silver writing that was elegant yet rugged. I took a tester of the cologne and sniffed it, smelling the luxurious scent inside. It was a little woodsy, though it had hints of other things in it too. I couldn't place my finger on it, but I knew that I liked it, and that I'd definitely like Blake to be wearing it.

"How much is this?" I asked, taking his attention from another browsing customer.

"Fifteen dollars for that size, twenty for the next up," he said.

"I'll take the fifteen-dollar one," I said, pulling out my wallet.

I didn't know if Blake would like it, let alone wear it for me, so I thought I'd just get him the smaller size and if he liked it, get him a bigger one when he ran out. I thought it'd be up his alley since he usually had a woodsy scent to him, but it was always best to be safe.

The man pulled out a box of it, wrapped it up for me, and I handed him a ten and a five before he smiled and handed me the bag. Nicolette came up, poked her head about, and snooped through my bag to see what I'd bought.

"It's cologne," I said, swatting her hand away.

"Ohh, how sweet. Buying him a scent you like, huh? The mark of a relationship," she said.

"I like his other scents, but I just thought this one would be nice to add to the collection. Besides, it's about time I surprise him with something I got with my own money," I said.

"That's nice of you. Want to make our way out of here? I'm starting to feel cramped," Nicolette said.

"Yes, please. I've been ready since we got here," I said.

With our hands clutching our purses in front of us, we pushed and shoved our way through the crowds who were doing exactly the same thing. I felt like a fish inside a crowded aquarium. This stressed me out and I was about to escape, so I couldn't imagine how fish felt, trapped in their tanks.

We went through a few doors before getting outside and finally being able to stretch our arms and legs a bit. People were still coming in, and there was a line of them buying tickets. Nicolette took out her phone and found a place nearby where we could go and get some coffee so that we didn't have to be boring and go home already.

The café, which was about five minutes away, was fairly empty as we walked in to the aroma of coffee and the sight of dozens of pastries protected inside a glass case. I salivated at the sight, even though I'd just eaten, and got a blueberry muffin with my coffee just because.

I watched as the barista, a cute guy Nic was trying to flirt with, put a little design in her coffee, a flower, before he gave us our drinks and snacks.

We walked over to a small two-person table against the glass and unwrapped our muffins as little bits crumbled out from underneath. I picked one of the blue-stained pastries up and popped it in my mouth before feeling the buttery, smooth texture melt against my tongue. I wasn't expecting it to still be this fresh this late in the day.

"So, tell me more about what Blake is up to in Seattle," Nicolette said.

"You guys are opening another office, aren't you?" I asked.

"Yeah, I think I heard about that, but I'm not really in the grapevine with that sort of stuff. It's not like they were heavily advertising it to us," she said.

"That's strange. You'd think they'd want to see if anybody wanted to transfer and help train people up there," I said.

"Yeah, maybe they did, but not me," she said, laughing.

"Oh hush, you do a great job," I said.

"I do a decent job, but I'm not the best at training people. My mind works kind of differently, you know? It's hard for me to explain to people how to do something. I'd be a mess of a teacher," she said.

"I can't wait to go and see his hometown," I said.

"That's a huge step. I'm so happy you guys are taking it," she said.

"I can't tell if he's nervous at all. I don't think that it's about me going there, though. I think he's just nervous about being back there," I said.

"Most people are when they visit home again. I would be if I were in his shoes, going back to that tiny town and seeing people who were a dick to me growing up," she said.

"Yeah, but look at him now. It's not like they'd be that way today," I said.

"I know that, but seeing them can bring back those memories and feelings. Bullies can really have a hold on you even later in life. Being traumatized as a child can have long effects," she said.

"I guess you're right. He did mention he doesn't have many friends there—at least not that he wants to see," I said.

"I wonder why," she said, looking at me.

"Oh," I said as my phone buzzed in my purse.

I pulled it out, seeing that Blake had sent me something before unlocking my phone and looking at the message. It was a photo of him at the new office, his smiling face putting me in an even better mood than I was in. There was something about just seeing his face, especially seeing him smiling, that did a number on me.

"That him?" Nicolette asked.

"Yeah, a picture of him at the new office," I said as I typed a reply.

"I'm surprised you didn't go with," she said.

"He would've been too busy and I have school and stuff. It just wasn't good timing," I said.

"How's that going?" she asked.

"What? School?" I asked, and she nodded. "It's going well, I suppose. As well as it can. I'm just counting down the days until I'm out of there and never have to take another test or turn in another assignment again."

"I was the same way. You'll still have assignments, especially in your field, but I guess they won't quite be the same. The good part is that you'll get paid to turn them in instead of you paying the school to *get* to turn them in. I'll be remembering that for a while, with how much my loans are," she said.

"Yeah, you're telling me. I wish I could've been born into a rich family who would've fronted the entire bill," I said with a chuckle.

"Your and Blake's children will. That's a plus," she said.

I choked a little on my coffee as I set it down and put my mouth into my sleeve.

"That's taking it a little far, don't you think?" I asked before composing myself.

"Oh, come on, you really think there's a chance you two won't end up together forever? Please. This is more than just some fling or fun time dating each other. This is love, baby, and it's real. I can tell just by looking at you," she said.

I sat there picking apart my muffin as I tried to deter any more questions on the subject. It wasn't that I was ashamed, by any stretch of the imagination, but after everything Blake and I had been through I just wanted to leave that subject alone for now.

"Do you?" she asked, after about thirty seconds of me not talking.

"What?" I replied.

"Love him," she said.

My heart started to race as I felt my palms become clammy and my face grew warm. I knew she wasn't going to let the subject go anytime soon, and I also knew I could trust her with whatever answer I gave her. Did I love Blake? Sure I did, but was I *in love* with him? There's a huge difference between those two things, and I wasn't fully sure about the second one.

I knew that I loved being around him. I knew that I missed him terribly either when he was gone or just simply when we were apart. I couldn't get enough of him when we were together, and although we'd been through the wringer, I wouldn't have had it any other way. It had formed and shaped us to where we were now. After thinking of all these things, the answer seemed pretty clear to me. The only question was if he felt all those same ways about me.

"I think so," I said.

Nicolette beamed with excitement and grabbed my hands as I exhaled a little and finally let it out. I was in love with him. I was in love with Blake Hunter.

CHAPTER SIXTEEN

Blake

The day had nearly come for our trip to my hometown and I was more excited and nervous than I'd been in a while.

It was the day before and we were getting our things ready last-minute for the trip. I hadn't a clue what to expect when we got there, and my mother stupidly leaked the secret of our arrival to someone in town, who told another person, who then told their cousin, and so on and so forth. All of a sudden the entire town wanted to see us and say hello. That wasn't what I'd planned, that was for sure.

That was part of the reason I didn't tell my mother what time we were flying in or where we were coming from. I knew she meant well, and she didn't mean anything malicious at all, but the last thing I needed was to be rushed when I got off the plane by people who were too overly excited to see me, and not really for the reasons I'd want.

Penny had a mid-term earlier in the morning, so we planned for an eleven a.m. flight out that would take a few hours. We'd get there around three their time, maybe a little later, which was perfect. No awkwardness of sitting around all day, and it was close enough to dinner that I knew my mother would want to do something almost right after we got there. The early bird special doesn't last all night, you know.

All the travel plans aside, I was just happy that work wasn't going to keep me too preoccupied. The Seattle branch was open and running, the merger was about done, and I had Grace move everything around so that I would be good to go. I made it abundantly clear to my *entire* staff not to bother me unless it was important. Even then, they shouldn't call me unless it was threatening to the business. Texts and emails were otherwise okay. I had to reiterate my point a few times over the last few days, but I was dead serious and I wasn't going to tolerate insolence. This trip was important not just to me, but to us.

Penny was going to spend the night tonight and have Gustav drive her to and from her school tomorrow morning so that we could save time and not miss our flight, though I guess they weren't going to leave without me. I did charter it, after all.

"Okay, is everything squared away?" I asked as Grace came into my office for our end of the day update.

"Yes, sir, everything is ready for you. Will you be

needing any airport information?" Grace asked.

"Send it to Gustav, please. It won't do me any good. The board is ready for my departure?" I asked.

"Yes, I asked earlier and they said that they will be fine to hold everything down until your return. They also fully understand your contact policy," she said.

"Good. Well, I suppose I'll see you in a few days then. Contact me if anything important happens, or if there's a coup," I said, smiling.

"Will do, Mr. Hunter," she said before leaving the office.

I grabbed the rest of my things, locked everything up, and headed out the door and to my waiting car before screeching out of the parking garage and towards home, where I'd soon meet Penny.

"I missed you," Penny said as she jumped into my arms.

She nuzzled her face into my shoulder as the rosy smell of her hair wafted up into my nostrils. I loved being around her, and I knew that the next few days were going to be great, even if they wouldn't be perfect.

"I missed you too. Are you all packed?" I asked, even though I saw her suitcases.

"Yeah, but I keep getting the feeling that I'm forgetting something. It always happens before a trip anywhere. I need to start making lists before I leave," she said.

"I told you that the other day. Oh well, we can always get you something when we're there if you forgot something. There are some chain stores about twenty or so minutes away from town," I said as I set her down.

"Have you eaten yet?" she asked.

"Not yet. I had a pizza made for us earlier. Just have to cook it," I said.

"Good. I'm starved," she said.

I turned on the oven and poured us some wine before handing her glass to her and clinking them together.

"Here's to us," I said, with our glasses raised.

"To us. Hopefully many more trips after this as well," she said.

We walked over to the couch after sipping our wine and set our glasses down on the coffee table before she cuddled up to me in the cutest way and refused to let go. I ran my fingers through her hair, looking down at her every once in a while, though not letting her catch me looking.

I couldn't believe I was finally going to take a girl home after all this time. It had been a while since I had, and that time hadn't had the best outcome. I knew that Penny was nothing like her, and that our relationship was much, much better, but I couldn't help but feel a little worried. My home didn't exactly have the cheeriest of memories anyway, so tossing that on top was almost a little too much.

The oven beeped and I pried her away enough to get up and put the pizza in. It needed twenty minutes, which felt like forever when you're hungry, but I suppose we didn't have another choice.

"I know we haven't gone yet, but thank you," she said as she came up beside me.

"For what?" I asked.

"For bringing me along with you. For trusting me enough to let me meet your family and friends and all that. It means a lot," she said as she looked up at me with glistening eyes.

"Anything for you," I said, kissing her forehead and seeing a little smile come across her face.

I knew things wouldn't be perfect this weekend, but it was bound to happen sometime, and all I could do at the end of the day was make the best of it.

CHAPTER SEVENTEEN

Penelope

"And please bring your exam up front when you're finished. You may leave after that, thank you," my professor said before handing out our exams.

I was completely ready for it, having studied a bit beforehand and knowing as much as I could know about all the material we went over so far in the semester. She even gave us a study guide that I wrote on, looked over, and kept with me for the past week. I don't know why I worried so much, or why I even studied this hard when I only had a few weeks left of school, but I guess I just wanted to do the best I possibly could.

She handed me the exam. It was four pages front and back, stapled together, though there were only about eight questions per page, so it wasn't so bad. I picked up my mechanical pencil, clicked out some lead, and wrote my name before I read the first question and confidently scribbled in my answer. It had been one of the first ones on my study guide, and was verbatim the same exact question. Were they all going to be this easy?

I flipped a page, and another page, and finally scribbled and filled in some more answers before I hit the last page, where there was an essay question. I was easily the furthest along in the class, and as I read the question, I tried to think of what I should write. I sucked at essay questions, and I knew that they were meant for critical thinking, but they never seemed to matter in the real world. I guess that's most of school, though. It's there to enlighten you, but it doesn't always teach you things you'll actually need. I was still waiting to use all the algebra I'd learned. Not sure it would ever happen.

I wrote in some bullshit answer, though I suppose it sounded okay, and put away my things before getting up at the same time as another kid and taking my test to the teacher. She smiled, nodding as I set down my exam. I slung my bag over my shoulder before walking out into the hallway and texting Blake that I was done with school and ready to go. He replied quickly, saying that Gustav would be there in a few minutes, and I walked out front and waited a short time before he pulled around and I got into the car.

Blake was still at his apartment, but he said he'd meet us with the bags downstairs so that we could leave right away. True to his word, he was standing in the garage as we pulled in, and he and Gustav put our bags in the trunk before Blake got in the car and kissed me hello.

"Ready for the trip of a lifetime?" he asked.

"Of a lifetime, huh? I suppose I am," I said, smiling.

"After you meet some of these people you might be wishing it's a trip that will only happen once in your lifetime," he replied before buckling his seatbelt.

"Oh, it won't be that bad," I said.

"Gustav, you've met my mother before. What did you think?" Blake asked.

"Well, she's lovely," Gustav said.

"What do you *really* think?" Blake asked.

"She's a little out there," Gustav quickly replied, causing Blake to smile.

"See, I told you. She means well, I think, but she can be a little much sometimes. Just warning you," Blake said.

Gustav pulled out of the garage and towards the airport as I looked out the window, trying to mentally prepare myself for the trip. I wasn't nervous because of what Blake said, but more about just meeting his family. It was a huge step, but I knew I was ready to take it and move on to the next chapter in our relationship.

The jet sat on the tarmac and as Gustav pulled around to it, someone standing there opened my door and helped me out of the back seat. Blake got out on his side, and Gustav opened the trunk and pulled out the bags as two airport workers grabbed them and stowed them on board for us. Blake shook the pilots' hands, I smiled and nodded, and we got on board, where the plush leather seats were waiting for our butts.

"I still can't get over how nice this is," I said as I ran my hand along the softened leather.

"Just imagine being in one of those itchy seats in coach and then look at this. It's amazing, isn't it? I make sure to say my prayers every time I get to fly like this. It could've been a lot different," he said.

I quickly became nervous once the engines started to roar and we began our taxi as we waited for lift-off. I tried to be tough, grimacing through it, but I knew Blake could see right through me and see how much of a little girl I was being. Hopefully I'd get better with time, but if not, at least I was on a private jet and not stuffed like a sardine in some flying tube with two hundred other miserable souls.

Our flight was rather uneventful, and as we got closer to Iowa, I looked out the window to see snow-covered patches of cornfields below. They didn't seem to end no matter how far we flew. We were definitely in the Midwest.

After circling around to get into position, the plane landed at a small airport that didn't have much in terms of either buildings or amenities. It wasn't a private airport, at least in the traditional sense of private back in San Francisco, but we had the privilege of having nobody else around aside from a few workers.

The plane taxied and the door opened before we walked out into air that was much more frigid than when we left a few hours ago. I saw my breath in front of me as I zipped up my jacket a little bit more and slipped my mittens on. A car, already on, sat nearby for us. The flight crew said goodbye and that they'd see us again in a few days. Blake walked around to the passenger side of the car and opened the door for me before helping me in and closing it behind me. I felt the warm leather seats against my cold butt as I looked down to see the seat warmers on their highest setting.

A cold breeze shot inside when Blake got in the car, but quickly subsided once he closed his door behind him.

"How far away are we from your parents' house?" I asked.

"About fifteen or twenty minutes. It isn't too far. I know the way," he said, and we buckled ourselves in and he pulled out of the tarmac and off the airport property.

I got glimpses of a landscape like my own hometown as we drove down a narrow country road through empty cornfields towards his childhood home. It seemed like most of the Midwest was like this, all barren and agricultural, but I guess that was what made this place home. I always hated it growing up, but now that I'd been away from it for so long, I sort of enjoyed seeing it again. It made me feel like I was home even though I wasn't.

After about twenty minutes of driving, we drove into a small town that didn't have much in terms of activity. Some people were outside working, others walking around, but the small area didn't have much else in terms of hustle and bustle. It was a far cry from

San Francisco, and a farther cry from what I thought it would be like.

People looked at our car, a large black SUV, as we drove through town like we were the president's motorcade coming through. They didn't wave, not even looking all that friendly, but perhaps that was because we were outsiders in their tiny town and they didn't know who we were.

After turning down a few streets, we pulled up to a house and Blake pulled into the driveway, put the car in park, and turned it off. We were here.

CHAPTER EIGHTEEN

Blake

I could see my mother in the window smiling from ear to ear as I got out of the car and planted my feet firmly on the driveway. I walked around to the trunk, opened it, and pulled our luggage out of the back before Penny came around and helped me with it.

"I saw her in the window," I whispered, since I didn't know if she had the door open or not.

"She's just excited to see you," she whispered back before I closed the trunk.

I walked around and as we walked up the driveway, my mother opened the front door of their small ranch and greeted me with a big hug and tons of smiles.

"I'm so happy you came, Blake," she said as she

swayed from side to side.

"I'm happy to see you too, Mom," I said with a smile.

"And who might this be?" she asked, smiling, as she pushed her glasses back up her nose.

"Mom, this is Penny, my girlfriend. Penny, this is my mother, Wendy," I said.

"It's nice to meet you, Mrs. Hunter," Penny said politely.

"Oh please, my name is Wendy. Mrs. Hunter is my husband's mother," she said, giving Penny a hug.

"Is Dad around?" I asked as I looked inside the living room.

"Of course I'm around. I live here, don't I?" my father asked as he came out from around the corner and greeted me with a handshake.

That was typical of my father—not giving me hugs and instead just shaking my hand like a real man, or at least that was his reasoning. Hugs were for your momma and your daughter, but not for your son.

"Earl, this is Penny, Blake's girlfriend," my mother said.

"Nice to meet you. I hope your flight was all right," my father said.

"Let's get you two out of the cold before we get all chit-chatty," my mother said, as we'd left the door open to the cold winter breeze.

We closed the door and took off our snowy shoes before my father helped me take our bags to my old room, which was just the way I'd left it. I had a few sports trophies on my dresser, though nothing spectacular, as I wasn't the most coordinated when it came to that kind of stuff. I was just lucky to be on some winning teams, even though I didn't contribute much to us winning those trophies.

As my father left the room I looked around for a second and smelled the air. It had this distinct smell that I'd never been able to place. It wasn't a particular smell, at least I didn't think so, but this house had smelled the same way all my life and likely long before I was born, and when I smelled it, I knew that I was home.

"Did you see anybody on the way in?" my mother asked as I walked back into the foyer.

"Nope, just a bunch of townies looking at the car like we were aliens," I said.

"Well, look at that thing! No wonder they did," my father said, looking out the window at the car.

"It's what they had available for us. We didn't pick it," I said.

"Should've gotten yourself a truck. That's what I would've done," he said.

"This is a lovely home you've got," Penny said, sensing that I was getting uncomfortable.

"Well, thank you, dear. It isn't much, but what we have is mighty special," my mother replied.

"Well, I love it," Penny replied with a smile.

"Is dinner coming soon? Or do we have plans?" I asked.

"Oh, I thought we'd go to the diner for fish, if that's okay," my mother said.

"That's fine, Mom. We can go anywhere you want to go," I said.

"How about we leave in about forty-five minutes? That'll give you guys time to unpack and freshen up before we leave," she said.

"Sounds good. We'll go do that now," I said, leaning in and giving her a peck on the cheek.

As Penny and I walked away towards the bedroom, I already felt the tension building with every step. I wasn't looking forward to going out. Not here.

CHAPTER NINETEEN

Penelope

There was a certain charm to Blake's family that I think he didn't like to talk about. I could sense he was a little uncomfortable, but I think that's sometimes to be expected when you go back home after being away for so long. While his mother was fairly warm and loving, at least from what I saw, his father was much, much different. It was easy to see that Blake didn't receive the attention he wanted from him growing up, and maybe that was a small part of the reason why he sometimes acted the way he did.

"How many drawers do you need?" Blake asked as we opened our suitcases.

"One should be fine. I don't have all too much with me," I said as I began to take out my clothes.

"I'm sorry for that out there," he said in a softer

voice.

"For what?" I asked.

"The way they are. I know they can be a bit... *much*," he said.

"They're fine," I said, smiling to reassure him.

"Just making sure. I've never really done this—showing them off and letting people in my life meet them. Most people would think they're too country, you know?" he asked.

"I'm from Illinois, so I know how people like this can be. I wasn't raised in some country club mansion, remember," I said, leaning in and giving him a kiss on the cheek.

"I know you weren't. Thankfully," he said.

We put our clothes away and zipped up our suitcases before putting them in the closet. Blake let me freshen up if I wanted to, but he told me I didn't need to get dressed up for where we were going. It wasn't the kind of place where you needed to wear anything nice.

I went into the bathroom with my toiletry bag and put on a little more makeup before changing into a nice blue sweater and jeans that I'd gotten not too long ago. I kept my hair down, mostly because I'd just washed it earlier and it wasn't looking greasy, and came out to see Blake had changed into a sweater and slacks of his own.

"You look nice," I said with a smile as I set down my things.

"I try not to wear a suit when I'm here. It's too Hollywood for them," he said, smiling.

"We live in San Francisco," I said.

"I know," he said, smiling again.

"Are you two just about ready? We need to head out before we miss our table," his mother said from outside.

"I take it this is a happening place?" I asked.

"For this town, yes," he said.

All eyes were on us as we walked into the slightly crowded diner. It wasn't too bad, about a third of the tables were still open, but it was the liveliest place I'd seen in this town so far. People got up from their tables, smiles on their faces, as they walked up and shook our hands like we were the Kennedys. I just went along with it as some of the older women hugged Blake and pinched his cheeks like they were his grandmothers. It was sweet seeing how he just went along with it and didn't push them away, instead reciprocating their love and kindness. I didn't think I'd seen this from him at home.

"My, my, Mr. Blake Hunter, how are you, son?" a man with suspenders that kept his blue jeans just below his potbelly said as he walked from the back.

"Hello, Harold, it's nice to see you," Blake said as he extended his hand.

"Oh come now, we're basically family! Give me a hug!" he said before giving Blake a hug.

"This is Harold, the owner of the diner and some other places in town. Harold, this is my girlfriend, Penny," Blake said, introducing me.

"Well hello there, beautiful," Harold said, as he grabbed my hands and spun me around.

"Watch yourself," Blake said in a playful tone.

"You picked yourself a beauty there, Blakey, that's for sure. So, are you guys here for supper?" Harold asked.

"You betcha," Earl said, clutching his stomach.

"Well, let's get you guys a table and some drinks," Harold said, grabbing four menus and guiding us to a corner booth, which must've been treasured with the way Blake's mother acted when we got it.

"Look over the menu, we made some changes since last time, and I'll go get you guys some water before you order," Harold said, knocking on the end of the table and walking away.

I opened my menu and was met with all the normal items you'd get at any small-town diner anywhere in the Midwest. I knew Wendy wanted the fish fry, and I planned on going along with her and getting it, but I couldn't help looking over everything else. I missed this type of food sometimes. You just couldn't get it back in San Francisco.

"I can smell that fish cooking right in back," Earl said, a toothpick hanging out of his mouth.

"It brings back a lot of memories," Blake said.

"Remember the time you just had to know how they cook that fish? He was about five or six, waist high, and he just wouldn't relent," Wendy said, laughing, as she talked to me. "He said, 'Mama, I want to see them make the fish,' and Harold finally relented and took him in the back and let him make the fish for our entire table. Well, that was sweet and all, but it definitely wasn't cooked or prepared like usual, let's just say."

"I put too much batter on and didn't fry it long enough," Blake said.

"It was like biting into a fresh raw fish," Wendy said, her face red.

"That's so cute," I said, smiling.

"We've got pictures at home, whole albums, and I'll have to make sure to pull them out," Wendy said.

"I'd love to see a young Blake running around," I said, smiling.

"Okay, folks, I've got your waters here. You know what you want or do you want some more time?" Harold asked.

"Are we all doing the fish fry?" Wendy asked.

I nodded and Blake did as well before Harold wrote down our order. Earl also ordered a beer, the same as Blake, and Wendy and I both got diet sodas, even though I didn't drink it all that often.

I watched as servers brought out the fish dinners to other patrons around us. I could feel the saliva wanting to drip out of my mouth, watching as the golden brown coating on the fish still bubbled with little drops of frying oil. It also came with cole slaw, a biscuit, and fries, and boy was it a lot of food for such a low price. The sign out front said it was $7.99 for the entire thing.

A woman brought our drinks by and set them all down. Earl took a big swig of his beer and licked the froth from his upper lip.

"That's a damn good brew," he said as he looked

at it affectionately.

I could tell Blake wasn't a huge fan of it, but I suppose his taste buds were a little more refined now in comparison to his father's. As we sat there taking sips from our drinks without much to say, I could see some of the people in the restaurant looking over at us and smiling. Well, I guess they were looking at Blake and not us, since we likely didn't matter much to them. It was sort of awkward, but it wasn't something I hadn't faced before with him.

"So, you guys are doing all right? You've been getting what I send for you?" Blake asked.

"What stuff?" Wendy asked.

"You know, Mom, the help I send. The clothes, food, medicine, things like that," Blake said.

His father nodded a little, as if saying don't bother, but his mother looked a little confused and not quite all there. I was a little confused too, but I didn't say anything to either Blake or his father. Was this the kind of stuff Blake had told me about? Was he ashamed of this for some reason?

"Oh, I forgot to thank you for the packages you sent," Wendy said out of the blue about five minutes later.

"I'm glad you liked them, Mom. Did they make you happy?" he asked.

"Oh, so much so!" Wendy said, just before a waitress came with our food.

"We have four fish dinners here," she said, starting to set them down in front of us.

I saw the sizzle of those same grease bubbles on the outside of my filets. The little cup of tartar sauce was beautifully white and a little curl of the sauce on top brought it all together.

I picked up my fork and stuck it in the cole slaw. The somewhat watery sauce dripped from my fork and down over the fish as I brought it to my mouth. I took a bite, tasting the cold, vinegary snap that reminded me of my own home. This was the exact way they made it there. Hell, I might as well be eating there.

"Just like I remember it," Blake said as he took a bite of the fish covered in tartar sauce.

"Blakey has always loved a lot of tartar on his fish. He won't eat it any other way!" Wendy said as she cut her fish into smaller pieces.

"Can I get another cold one?" Earl asked before letting out a small burp to the side.

Dinner went off without a hitch, though Wendy didn't act strangely any more during the meal. I wondered if she'd had a brain fart or if there was something wrong with her that Blake forgot to mention. I knew she wasn't the best mother in the world, at least according to him, but was this the reason why? I knew I'd have to bring it up to him later tonight, even if it was going to be a little uncomfortable.

A few people came up to the table while we were there and shook Blake's hand. They were old classmates, neighbors, and just general townspeople who knew and loved Blake and what he'd become. It was weird seeing all these people adore him, but I couldn't say I blamed them. I adored him a lot more.

The sun had already fallen when we walked out

of the restaurant, though I guess it was setting when we were walking in. One horrible thing about the winter months is how early day becomes night. It didn't seem to matter if you were on the chilly open plains or in the cool San Francisco bay.

Harold thanked us many times for coming in and said he wanted to see us again sometime before we left. Blake agreed, and took a picture with him for his wall of celebrities, which admittedly only had one other person on it, a low-rate country music singer nobody had ever heard of, and we walked back to the SUV.

The seat warmers came on strong as Wendy and I sat in the back seat and I rubbed my hands together. A few snowflakes started falling. Earl said a storm was rolling in and we'd better get home before she hit.

The roads were about as busy as they could get, which admittedly wasn't all that busy, though Blake navigated them without a hitch and we pulled back into the driveway just as the wind started to pick up and blow the snow around even more.

"How about we get inside and start a fire," Earl said as he unbuckled his seatbelt.

"Sounds like a good night to me," Wendy said.

As we got out of the car and walked up to the front door, Wendy picked up a small note from the neighbors saying that they heard Blake was in town and they hoped we'd all stop by sometime before he left. They unlocked the door, we walked in, and Wendy immediately played with the thermostat and turned the temperature up two degrees.

Our shoes, which were a little snowy and wet, sat

at the front door as the snow started to slowly melt off them with every passing minute. I was happy to be wearing a sweater, and as we sat down on their big leather couch, Blake pulled down a blanket and put it on top of the two of us. Wendy and Earl both had big recliners, and Earl turned on the news to see that there had been a school shooting in Des Moines earlier today.

"Shame, that is," he said, grabbing a bowl of pork rinds that were near the table and starting to munch on them.

"Earl Hunter, you just had a big dinner at the diner and now you're eating more? The doctor said you need to hold off," Wendy said.

"Eh, screw him. I know what's good for me," he said, brushing her off.

"If the doctor says so, you should listen to him," Blake said.

"I definitely don't need no sass from you, young man. I'm fine and perfectly healthy and that's that," Earl said, his gaze still on the television, though he didn't miss a beat.

Blake shook his head and held my hand underneath the blankets as Wendy insisted we turn something fun on that we all could enjoy instead of the news. Earl relented, and Wendy turned on some movie channel that was playing a classic that I'd never heard of, and quite frankly, I was glad I hadn't heard of it before now. Still, Blake and I didn't say a word and instead we just enjoyed the company.

After watching the movie, which ended around nine, Wendy and Earl said that they were going to get to bed. We said our goodnights, and as they walked away and I knew they weren't going to be coming back, I knew it was time to ask Blake what went on with his mother earlier.

"So, I have a question for you," I said as he flipped through the channels.

"What's up?" he asked.

"What happened at dinner earlier?" I asked.

"What do you mean?" he replied.

"When your mom, you know, forgot," I said.

"Oh, that," he said.

I watched the expression on his face as it turned a little sour and I could tell it was something he was uncomfortable with. I didn't want to push him or anything, but I felt that maybe I should know since I was here with him. He could trust me.

"For the past few years she's had some problems remembering short-term things. The doctor said it's likely early dementia, though it isn't bad now or anything like that. First it just started off forgetting easy things, like grocery lists and basic news and stuff like that. It's now progressed to where she has a lot of her long-term memory there, but not so much recent things. She's getting treated for it, and they're doing anything and everything they can, but yeah, she's not all there," he said.

"I'm very sorry to hear that. How are you holding up?" I asked.

"About as well as I can, I guess. I was never super close to my parents, but I still don't want to see them suffer or go through any diseases or problems. They're still my parents no matter what, and I'm more than willing to get them the care and medication they need. I just hope that it doesn't all go away anytime soon. What happens when her long-term memory vanishes? Will there be any shred of her left?" Blake asked.

"That's a tough question to answer," I replied.

"Hopefully I'll get an answer, and hopefully it will be one that I want to hear. I know that while my father loves her and takes care of her the best he can, it would be extremely hard to care for someone who can't do anything for themselves or remember anything, especially considering he isn't the most capable or fit man himself. He's got a whole host of medical problems that could make it near impossible for him to care for himself in ten years, much less his wife," Blake said.

"I know it's probably hard not to, but I'd just say to not worry about it so much. It's out of your hands, and at the end of the day all you can do is give them the treatment they need and hope for the best. Worrying about it and stressing out over it won't do any good and won't change the outcome for better or worse," I said.

"You're right," he said, squeezing my hand a little.

"Better?" I asked.

"Yeah. Thank you for being you," he said, leaning in and giving me a kiss.

We continued to watch a little more TV as I could hear the wind howling outside. I looked out the window and saw snowdrifts forming as their back deck lights shone over the yard and illuminated the crystal-like flakes. They looked beautiful—like diamonds flying around in the night sky as Blake held me close and kept me warm. This trip wasn't so bad after all.

CHAPTER TWENTY

Blake

I hated running into people I knew from high school more than anything in the world.

High school wasn't a particularly good time for me, though it wasn't quite the worst, either. I'd say that I got picked on, most kids did, and now that I had the money and status that I did, it seemed like everyone, including my old bullies, were my very best friends in the world. I didn't know if they expected money or presents or whatever, but you'd think that we were twins separated at birth.

Today wasn't any different as we walked through the aisles of the Walmart that was about twenty minutes from my parents' house. It was the only one in the area and where everyone from an hour around congregated to do their main grocery shopping and just general shopping. My parents were no different, and they dragged us here so that we could get some things and check out the area a bit more. This town had much more to offer, including a small mall and a movie theatre, though they weren't exactly a huge draw. I guess if you lived around here they were great.

"Blake?" I heard asked from behind me.

I turned around to see Aaron, a guy a year older than me who used to live a couple blocks away. He was a real dick. He used to shove my head out of the bus window and make me flinch so that he got to hit me. That was a big thing when I was in school. People would make you flinch or make some stupid circle symbol with their hand below their waist and if you flinched or looked at the symbol they'd get to hit you in the shoulder. My entire tenth year on this earth involved a black and blue shoulder. I bet he didn't remember that, though.

"Hello, Aaron," I said with an almost melancholic and pained tone.

That didn't seem to get through to him, though, as he shook my hand with a huge shit-eating grin and said hi to my parents, who I knew he must've seen every now and again around town.

"How are you, Aaron?" my mother asked.

"Oh I'm good, Mrs. Hunter. I didn't know Blake was back in town. How long are you here for?" Aaron asked.

"Just a couple more days. Figured I'd come see my parents and spend some time with them before work picks back up," I said, as I knew to just bullshit myself around people like him.

I definitely wasn't afraid of him anymore, and he obviously wouldn't try anything on me these days, but I never forgot the person he was when we were younger. I knew people would try to tell me he was a kid and kids do stupid and crazy things sometimes, but for some reason I just didn't care about those excuses. He might've changed, and maybe he hadn't bullied or hurt anybody in a very long time, but he did bully and hurt me, and I'd never forget it as long as I lived.

"We're gonna have to go get a beer or something! I'd love to catch up," Aaron said.

"That's a great idea, Aaron," my mother said, not helping as usual.

"Yeah, I'll check my schedule and get in touch with you. You still around town?" I asked, both to ask him and to sort of make a dig at him.

"Yup, still around. Took over the towing business dad had. Going well," he said, as chipper as can be.

"That's awesome. Glad to hear it," I said with a fake smile.

Maybe if my parents and Penny hadn't been around I would've blown him off or acted differently, but instead I bit my tongue and kept polite. I didn't want to cause a scene and I didn't want to embarrass my parents, who still had to stay in this cesspool of a town and deal with the rumors and drama that would unfold from me being a dick to someone.

"Who is this?" he asked, looking at Penny.

"This is my girlfriend, Penny," I said.

"I knew little Blake when he was just a small guy.

Him and I were something fierce back in those days," Aaron said, his hands in his pockets.

"It's nice to meet you. I bet you were," she said, sensing my discomfort.

"Well, anyway, I better get going. I just stopped to pick up a few things. I mean it about that beer, Blake. I'd love to catch up," Aaron said.

"I'll stop on by sometime and let you know," I said with another fake smile.

"Okay, sounds good! See you guys!" Aaron said, and everyone said bye and I got to turn off my fake happiness.

"About damn time," my dad said, tossing the toothpick in his mouth around.

"I thought you liked him," I said.

"Not a chance. That kid's a dick," my father said.

"Earl!" my mother exclaimed.

"We were all thinkin' it, Wendy," he said before we started moving again.

I loved that my dad didn't have a filter, though I didn't always love it growing up. He was a little too honest sometimes, and although it shaped me into the person I was today, I couldn't help but wonder what I could've been molded into had he been more caring and thought about his words before he said them. I couldn't count the number of times he said something bad and my mother forced him to go apologize to me. There are some things in this world you just shouldn't say to a kid, and Earl Hunter said them all.

"Are ya'll getting hungry?" Wendy asked after we checked out and walked to the car.

"Yeah, I could eat," Penny said.

"That's a question you don't have to ask with me," my father said.

The clouds were dark even though there was no snow falling, and we all got into my SUV and drove down the street to some chain restaurant that was starting to fill up for lunch. The theme was Tex-Mex, and every entrée I saw as we walked to our table was covered in queso or heaps of deep-fried chips and potatoes. It wasn't my typical kind of place, but then again nothing around here was. None of this was even around when I was a kid, but I guess change is never a bad thing. The people around here loved it and that was all that mattered.

"Here you are. Your server is Paul and he'll be with you shortly," the hostess said with a smile before walking away.

Nobody had seemed to notice me here, which was a sign of good times to come. I wasn't a celebrity by any stretch of the imagination, but you'd think I was Brad Pitt or George Clooney around here. Hell, I'd probably get more attention than them if they were standing right next to me here.

"What looks good to you?" my mother asked as we looked over our menus.

"How about we get that chip platter for an appetizer?" my father asked.

"Do you guys like that?" my mother asked, looking at us over her menu.

"Yeah, that sounds great. I could go for some chips and salsa," Penny said.

"Blake?" my mother asked.

"Anything you guys want I'm fine with," I said.

"Hi guys, my name is Paul and I'll be your server today. Can I get you a house margarita or an app to start you off?" Paul asked as he set down small napkins for our drinks.

"Hi Paul, I think we're going to do the chip platter you have here," Wendy said as she pointed to it on the menu.

"Awesome choice, guys. That's definitely a fan favorite here. Can I start you off with anything to drink while they're working on that order?" he asked.

"I'll have a Coors Light," my father said.

"Just a diet coke with a lime for me, please," my mother said.

"I'll have the same as her," Penny said with a smile.

"Captain and Coke, please," I said.

"Great. I'll get all those in and be back shortly," Paul said before leaving.

"Captain and Coke, huh? At least you ain't drinking them girly drinks since moving out west," my father said.

"Oh be quiet, Earl. The boy can drink what he wants," my mother said, defending me like usual.

I kept to myself, sipping on my drink when it came, using the alcohol like a crutch to keep myself sane. I think things would be much better if I could just visit my mother.

We ordered our food and I got the fish tacos, extra spicy. Penny did the same, sans spice, and my mother pointed out how cute it was that we were ordering the same thing. She said she and my father used to be like that as well and always had to sit next to one another in booths and share all their food. I wondered what went wrong there. Obviously something major did.

As we sat waiting for our food, though, something—someone, rather, came up in the conversation out of nowhere. My heart dropped and I felt sick, a sour taste in my mouth. I knew it wasn't her fault, with her mind drifting and all, but I couldn't help feeling a bit anxious and scared as my mother mentioned her name.

"How's Lillian doing these days?" she asked.

I hadn't said that name, let alone thought about it in years. It was her name—the name of the woman who changed me forever. It was a secret and a curse that I hadn't even told Penny about, and I was very open with her. I could see the look on my father's face, one I didn't see often, as he gave me a bit of an "I'm sorry" expression. He knew what she said was out of bounds, but I couldn't be mad at her. It wasn't her fault.

"Who's Lillian?" Penny asked.

"His girlfriend," my mother said, as her mind must have drifted years back into the past.

Lillian had met my mother before, and the two of them surprisingly had hit it off to the point where my mother was determined to see us married. At that time it was great, and I thought we would get married, but the walls all came crashing down before I could even try to repair them.

I shook my head no to Penny as my mother ate some food and I tried to keep myself from sweating any more. Penny had an absolute look of bewilderment on her face.

"They aren't together anymore, remember?" my father said, with his arm around my mother. "It's been a few years since that happened. Okay?"

"It has? What happened? I like her," my mother said, with a glaze over her eyes that I couldn't be angry with.

"She did some bad things, Mom. How about you eat your lunch and we'll talk about it later, okay?" I asked.

"Okay, Blakey," she said with a smile, going back to her meal.

"Tell me about it later?" Penny whispered in my ear.

I nodded yes, but in my heart I was furiously shaking my head no. I didn't want to talk about Lillian for a very good reason. It wasn't that I didn't want to tell Penny or that I didn't trust her, it was just that it was painful to sit here and relive that experience. I knew that I was going to have to, though, and I wasn't sure I could fully prepare myself.

CHAPTER TWENTY-ONE

Penelope

I was quite curious about Blake and Lillian later, though I could tell he was very uneasy about it. I knew it was likely a sore subject for him, and that she'd hurt him or something, but I didn't think he had anything to be embarrassed about. He seemed like he thought I'd care, or that I'd be mad at either him or his mom even though I had no reason to be. We all have shitty exes, though by the way Blake had mentioned her in the past and even the way his dad stopped his mom, I was beginning to think their breakup was very bad.

Blake was fairly silent the rest of the day while we were out. His mother came to and didn't even remember bringing anything up. Well, nobody asked her or reminded her, but she didn't talk about the subject any longer and she knew who I was again, and that he wasn't dating some girl named Lillian. That was enough for a good assumption.

We went and saw a movie together, some comedy. As I looked over at Blake while holding his hand, he didn't seem like he was watching or enjoying much of the movie. His eyes were on the screen, but it was like they were on autopilot and he was just looking forward while his brain was doing something completely different. Did this woman really have *that* much of an effect on him that bringing her up or even saying her name would haunt him this much? It was sad to think about, but I guess Blake was kind of a different guy.

The movie let out and as the lights came on, Blake snapped out of his funk and took a deep breath in through his nose before looking at me.

"Okay?" I asked as we stood up.

"Yeah, I'm great," he replied, leaning in and giving me a peck on the forehead.

I brought the collar of my coat up to my mouth as we walked outside into the blinding white snow. The wind ripped against my cheeks and forehead as we shuffled through the parking lot. I could almost feel my face freezing so hard I was sure I was going to get frostbite. I definitely didn't miss that about the open Midwest plains.

The SUV was like a beacon in the snow as the glossy black exterior contrasted perfectly in the white parking lot. The seat warmers instantly turned on as Blake turned the key in the ignition and the air started to blow, albeit cold. We pulled out before anyone else left and made our way back to their house.

I checked the weather app on my phone as we drove back and saw that a storm with three to five inches was pulling through town. I didn't say anything, instead keeping quiet, as the mood was already quiet and filled only with the sound of the blowing wind outside.

Nobody was walking on Blake's street as we pulled onto it and up to his parents' house. Blake parked as far up the driveway as possible before we all got out and quickly walked up to the front door, where a flyer was stuck to the doorknob for some kind of neighborhood party. Earl pulled it off before unlocking the door and letting us all pile in.

"That's better," Wendy said as she stomped the snow off of her boots on the front mat.

The furnace was on, and as Wendy pressed the thermostat up one degree I felt the warmth against my cheeks and the tip of my nose. The blood was rushing all over my face, the almost frostbitten edges of my skin starting to feel incredibly warm even though they were still a little cold to the touch.

I was hoping that the storm wouldn't hold us back too much in terms of things to do. We left the day after tomorrow, and I wanted to get to know Wendy and Earl more, even if they weren't the most outgoing or personable people I'd ever met. They were Blake's parents, though, and that was enough of a reason to me to try to make an effort. Besides, I didn't know the next time I'd get a chance.

"I think I'm going to make some cocoa. Would

anybody else like some?" Wendy asked.

Blake and Earl said yes, and I got up and offered to help her in the kitchen. She kindly accepted, and I went to the cupboard she pointed to and pulled out the mix and marshmallows as she got the mugs ready. It was just the kind you mix with hot water, nothing special.

"I'd really love to see any photo albums you have. I know you showed me one the other day, but I'm not sure if you have any more," I said.

"Oh, we have tons! We can look at the pictures while we drink our cocoa. It'll be fun," Wendy said with a big smile.

Using an office-type water jug they had in the kitchen, Wendy pressed the red button and filled the mugs with hot water before handing them to me and letting me fill them with the powder and mix them up. The mugs were rather large, enough for a few standard-sized marshmallows, so I dropped a few in each one and took them to Earl and Blake.

"What are you going to do?" Blake asked.

"Look at some old albums with your mom. Hopefully I'll see your little baby butt," I said, smiling.

"Oh, Wendy took tons of those photos," Earl said.

Blake smiled before I went back and made my cocoa while Wendy rummaged through the front coat closet and pulled out a box. She had two albums in her hands, both of them powder blue but with different designs. We sat down at the dining room table and Wendy put on her glasses.

"This is the first one," she said, pushing the other one aside and opening the first one.

There was a cornucopia of pictures of Blake as a baby all the way up to a young man and everything in between. They had a good number of pictures of him —more than I thought they'd have, considering how he'd talked about his childhood. They weren't all smiles; sometimes he had frowns or just mad faces, but it showed another side to Blake that I really didn't know existed.

"This is the time we took him to Chicago. Boy, was that a trip! He was so afraid of the big buildings and would stumble on his own feet when he'd look up at them," Wendy said, laughing a little.

"They were pretty daunting when I was that young," Blake said.

"Here he is at his fifth birthday party," Wendy said.

"Is that the guy we saw at Walmart?" I asked, pointing to a kid who looked remarkably similar to him.

"Aaron? Yeah, that's him. Unfortunately he was at my party," Blake said.

"His mother made him invite all the neighborhood kids so that they wouldn't feel left out. Stupid, if you ask me, making your kid invite his bully to the party. I don't even think the brat brought a present," Earl said.

"I did it in hopes that it would bring them together and they could be friends. It obviously didn't work," Wendy said.

"It was a good sentiment, anyway," I said.

We flipped through the pages with smiles on our faces as I saw pictures of a naked Blake in the tub and him painted up like a rodeo clown. Even though Blake and his parents weren't the closest of families, it was really great seeing all the memories that they had saved of him. By the way Blake spoke before I got here I was expecting them to have nothing at all. Maybe his perception of them and the truth were a little skewed.

Not much more happened during the night, as the snow outside had started to pile up and kept us indoors. Wendy cooked a meatloaf, mashed potatoes, and green beans with one biscuit for each of us, as that was all she had left over.

As the night grew old and Wendy and Earl started talking about hitting the hay, I knew that was my chance to talk to Blake. I'd waited all day, wondering as I tried to think of what could have been so bad about what happened between him and Lillian. I hadn't a clue about her, but I knew I was about to find out. I just hoped it wasn't something so bad that I hoped I wouldn't have ever found out.

"I can tell you want to talk about it," he said as he poured us a cup of coffee.

"Do you blame me?" I asked as I stood at the kitchen bar counter.

"I'm not sure where to even begin. It happened so long ago and I've put it out of my mind for so long that it's frightening to think about reliving it," he said.

"Just start from the beginning. Who even is she?" I asked.

Blake took a sip of his coffee as the steam billowed upwards and then he took a deep breath.

"Lillian is somebody I dated a few years back. Actually, she was my only truly serious girlfriend before you, and I wish I'd never even met her. We met after I moved to San Francisco with the dream of starting a company. Like I said, we'd been together for a little while and things were going great—at least to me. I thought I was going to marry her one day, and even though things weren't amazing in our lives, and we didn't have much money, we had each other," he said.

"That all sounds great," I said.

"It was, and I think that was all she wanted. You see, Lillian wasn't exactly driven, which is funny because I am. Even though we were poor and didn't have a ton, I dreamt of starting a business—any business, and making it into a success. One day I came up with the idea of the app that would turn into RandomMeetX. I was so excited about it and told her all about my idea and how I wanted to quit my job and put everything into it. She was vehemently against it, and for good reason. I didn't have the money to put towards it, but I didn't care. I'd get a loan, venture capital, or anything else as long as it meant getting this started. She didn't see the dream happening, though. She told me it was a waste of time and money and that I was messing up our future for a hookup and dating app. I told her that wasn't the case, that I was doing this for us, but she didn't listen. I should also say that I was a much different person back then as well. I was a pushover, I did everything I was told, and quite honestly I probably wasn't fully ready to run the type of company I have now," he said.

"It sounds like she just didn't want you to do something you might regret," I said.

"That's just where the story begins, though. So anyway, things became rocky between us. I started the company, but I had to take on part-time freelancing work just to make enough to live. We'd grown distant, and soon one day of silence turned into two, into seven. I tried to make things work, and I tried to make it last, but she just wasn't having it. What used to be us being affectionate turned into her despising me and thinking I was a loser as I frantically did whatever I could to build and launch this business. I even brought in a friend, a business partner, Ned, to make it happen. No matter what I did, though, nothing ever seemed to be enough. She'd resent me and make fun of me and in turn that made me depressed and unable to do anything with this business I'd pumped so many hours and so many dollars into. After a while of not getting anywhere, Ned's own finances were running dry and he had to take on part-time work at a restaurant. I was still freelancing, but I could do that anywhere and had no problems there. I'd go to coffee shops and use their Wi-Fi as I worked back and forth between the business and freelancing work for money. I thought Ned was doing the same, but I was dead wrong," he said.

I sat on the edge of my seat as I listened to every word Blake said. I felt like I was in a movie, and I wished I had popcorn. The multitude of expressions on his face conveyed more about him than I'd ever seen before.

"One day I got done early with work and decided to try to surprise Lillian. I'd just gotten finished with a job and had some cash so I bought her some flowers, rented a movie, and got her favorite takeout even though I couldn't afford any for myself. I didn't care about eating, though, as long as she was happy and we could finally have a night together like we used to. I took the bus home to the shitty apartment we had and saw the lights on from the street. She was home and I knew I'd be able to surprise her. I snuck up the three flights of stairs to the apartment and unlocked the door with a smile on my face—though that smile would soon be gone. As the door flung open, I saw a sight that will forever be etched into my brain. Ned wasn't going to some job at a restaurant, instead he was on my bed with my girlfriend. I had no idea how long this had been going on, whether it was that night, all the time he had this *new* job, or even longer than that. She looked scared at first as he tried to apologize, but I wouldn't have any of it. I threw the things down on the floor and left the apartment in a hurry. That sparked something in me that night that I haven't been able to get away from since. My work ethic and control kicked into gear and I feel that I actually started the company that night. Within two weeks I was going live, and from there it grew exponentially. I was lucky that Ned never had any control or stock in the company, and even though Lillian tried contacting me multiple times to get me to talk to her, I didn't listen. I got on billboards, magazine covers, and even television shows. I had sex with women and used them to my own advantage without giving them the emotion that I'd lost so long ago. I didn't care about them and I think I wanted to leave them hurt and confused just like I'd been," he said.

"Are you still like that?" I asked.

"No, I'm not," he said.

"And why not? Why change all that after what was done to you?" I asked.

"Because I met you, Penny. You changed my life. You saved me. I know you won't do the things to me that she did, and I know that not all women are the same. I know I thought that way before, but I don't think it still," he said.

I always had a hunch that something with a woman did all this to him. He'd mentioned her before, but he never really *mentioned* her in a way that would give me any answers. I knew that some people would see what he did to other women as cruel, but I thought I understood it. He couldn't let anybody in. He didn't let them see his beautiful heart and instead engrossed himself in his work, filling his love life with one-night stands and nothing else. I changed all that, though. I somehow became the person who showed him that those things weren't enough and that he needed someone there to give him the care he deserved.

"I know you don't think that way. I know you really do care about me and that you know I would *never* do anything to hurt you like that. I know we haven't always had the healthiest relationship, but that's all in the past. I only have one question," I said.

"What?" he asked.

"How come your mother knows her so well?" I asked.

"Oh, that. We'd visited a couple times when we were still in the good phase. She and my mother got along, and they grew to like each other. That all changed when she cheated on me, and now my mother hates her, but I think when she mentioned Lillian she wasn't quite remembering that," he said.

"Just wanted to make sure," I said, smiling.

"So yeah, that's my secret. That's what I've been hiding for so long. It probably sounds stupid right now," he said.

"Not at all, Blake. I think you have every right to feel the way you do and I'm just glad that you've worked past it and don't let it control you any longer. You have me now, and that's all you need to worry about," I said as I grabbed his hand over the counter and held it firmly.

Still holding my hand, he walked around the peninsula and gave me a soft kiss, and I could feel my stomach filling with butterflies and fireworks. How did I, a small-town girl from Illinois, get so lucky with such a wonderful man like Blake? He was everything I ever wanted in a man and more, and I knew that we could stand the test of time no matter what. I couldn't wait to explore those times with him.

CHAPTER TWENTY-TWO

Blake

Saying goodbye to my parents was always bittersweet. Sometimes I wished that they lived a little closer to me, but I knew that they belonged here in this house, in this town, in this part of their life.

Penny and I had a good visit with them, and I couldn't believe how easily they took to her. My father even pulled me aside this morning as I was packing up and said I had a keeper. It wasn't that I didn't know that, but it was nice to hear it from him. My mother cried as I said goodbye and asked if we could stay just a little bit longer. I felt bad, knowing that she likely was truly sad about us leaving, but I promised her I'd come back and see her again soon. With her health, I knew I had to. How long would it be before she started forgetting who I was?

I was able to avoid saying goodbye to anybody in town as they all shoveled their driveways and played in the snow. There was something comforting about watching kids playing in big yards and fields compared to what the kids back in San Francisco were able to do. The only snow they got to play with had been driven on and walked over so many times it was black and muddy. Not here, though. A kid could really be a kid here.

The plane was ready and warming up as we pulled up in the SUV and had our bags taken out of the trunk and stowed away.

"The pilots are just about ready for takeoff," the flight attendant said as we walked up the stairs and into the jet.

"Feeling okay?" I asked Penny.

"I'm good as long as you're here," she said with a smile.

We sat down in our seats and buckled ourselves in as I could hear the pilots making final preparations. Before I knew it, the plane was being closed and the flight attendant, Sara, was getting herself strapped in at the pilots' recommendation.

We taxied the runway and took off, as no other planes were anywhere near the vicinity of this small Iowa airport. As we took off and soared through the air, I looked out the window and saw the open expanse of snow-covered cornfields as they turned into patches in the air. I sometimes still couldn't believe that everything in my life, all of this, was a result of this little town. It shaped me and molded me into the man I am today, and even though some outside forces throughout my life have continued to change me, I'm still just a small-town boy with big-city dreams.

I looked forward at Penny, her hands not quite as white or red any longer from gripping the armrests, and as she looked back up at me, her eyes opening, I felt a warm feeling inside my stomach and my chest.

I was the luckiest man in the world, and I knew it for a fact.

CHAPTER TWENTY-THREE

Penelope

Almost three months have passed and my life has changed in a way that I dreamt of for so long.

Just a few days ago I walked across the stage and received my diploma before switching the tassel on my hat and beaming with joy. The degree I'd worked so hard for all those years was finally mine, and with a job already lined up, I knew that things were looking bright.

My family, at least some of them, had come into town for the occasion and Blake finally got to meet them. I knew he was nervous, but I told him to just be himself and not to try to impress them. He did just that and they took to him so much that I was waiting for them to ask him when he was going to marry me.

Speaking of Blake, things couldn't be better with

him than they are at this very moment. I spend a lot more time at his place now, and I even have a space in his closet for a lot of my things. I wouldn't quite say I've moved in, or that I will anytime soon, but it's all good progress and I'm happy to have it.

We spend a lot more time together, and we've even gone on double dates with Nicolette and her new boyfriend, Edward. He isn't the most gorgeous man alive, at least not by her old standards, but he treats her like a queen and all she ever talks about are the butterflies he gives her and the cute things they do together.

As Blake and I walk onto his terrace as the falling summer sun fades into the distance, I can't help but feel like things in my life are finally coming together. I have my degree, a job, great friends, and the most amazing man in my life close to me.

"We've had a crazy ride, haven't we?" Blake asked as we sipped a glass of wine while watching the sunset.

"Yeah, the craziest. For a while there I wasn't sure we were going to make it," I said.

"I think I always knew we would," he said, looking at me with a smile.

"Oh yeah? How come?" I asked.

"Because when you love someone, you always make it work," he said.

My stomach dropped as my heart began to race and a million thoughts ran through my head. Did he really just say that? He'd come close once before, but he never once said that word to me like this.

"You love me?" I asked.

"Yeah, I do," he said, his gaze fixed on me.

I bit my lower lip, gripped my glass tighter, and finally said the words I'd been waiting to say for so damn long.

"I love you too."

Did you like this title? If so, please consider leaving a review. It will help not only me as the author grow, but will also let other readers know your thoughts and opinions.

Want to receive the first three volumes of my serial series The Stipulation for free? Sign up for my mailing list below and have them delivered right to your inbox. You'll receive new book notifications, free books, giveaways, and much more!

http://eepurl.com/bb6VVb

ABOUT THE AUTHOR

M.L. Young is a New Adult Romance author currently residing in northern Illinois. When not writing, she enjoys horseback riding, sewing, and dreaming about the hot guys she writes about in her books.

M.L. loves interacting with fans, so interact with her! You can find her on Facebook, Twitter, and through e-mail!

www.facebook.com/realmlyoung

www.twitter.com/realmlyoung

www.authormlyoung.com

Made in the USA
Lexington, KY
11 June 2017